TASTE OF CHANGE

A BLUE QUILL CHAPTER ANTHOLOGY

VIRGINIA BABCOCK   HOLLY CHILCOTT

M. C. ELAINE   J. ALAN GIFT   NANCY GRANDUCCI

KAM HADLEY   JO LYNNE HARLINE   TERRA LUFT

INNA V. LYON   SEPTEMBER ROBERTS   M. ROHR

VALARIE SCHENK   KEITH STEELE

D1739123

Blue Quill Chapter
League of Utah Writers

Taste of Change

Copyright 2023 by Blue Quill Chapter

bluequillutah@gmail.com

Cover art copyright 2023 Dracon Studios

ISBN: 9798864988558

"Gone Foraging" 2023 Jo Lynne Harline

"Liver and Onions" 2023 Keith Steele

"Spring Chicken" 2023 M.C. Elaine

"Kibble" 2023 Valarie Schenk

"Seagulls Saved Them Again" 2023 Kam Hadley

"From Russia with Borscht" 2023 Inna V. Lyon

"Hart and Soul" 2023 September Roberts

"Doors" 2023 J. Alan Gift

"Found In Transit" 2023 Holly Chilcott

"A Taste of Life" 2023 Nancy Granducci

"Blessed With Gas" 2023 Virginia Babcock

"Tempting Truths" 2023 Terra Luft

"The Good Girls Chemical High" 2023 M. Rohr

LEAGUE OF UTAH WRITERS

BLUE QUILL CHAPTER

The Blue Quill Club was founded on June 3rd, 1928. In 1937, when the League of Utah Writers was formed, the Blue Quill Club became the Blue Quill chapter, the League's oldest chapter. While many years have gone by and some things have changed, the core values of our writing group have remained the same. We, like other chapters of the League of Utah Writers, offer friendship, education, and encouragement to the writers and poets of Utah. While most of our members live in and around Ogden, we have members who travel for miles to join us. Everyone is welcome to attend our meetings. Whether you're interested in hearing from our guest speakers or participating in our critique groups, there's something for everyone in the Blue Quill chapter.

A Blue Quill Chapter Anthology

Book Five of Six

Taste of Change

Edited by Thoth Editing

CONTENTS

GONE FORAGING

JO LYNNE HARLINE

Poetry

To my relief, fried grasshoppers were not offered as
    waiters served our class a three-course sampler meal:
    first, a tender cattail leaves and spring onion salad,
    next, pot-roasted grouse with berries and pinion nuts,
    and last, roast venison and crisp, dried pumpkin seeds.
    We ate the samples with our fingers, seated in rows of
    folding chairs, and listened to an archaeology professor
    lecture about the diet of the Fremont Indians who once
    lived in this area of Utah from 400 A.D. to 1350 A.D.
    They fished, and they hunted for animals and birds,
    and went out foraging for roots, berries, nuts, and seeds.

After they became farmers, planting and harvesting corn
    in the early form of smaller ears of maize, it caused them
    some nutrition stress, as their teeth and bones have revealed
    in lab analysis, from over-dependence on the starchy maize.
    The Fremont learned to balance proteins with other foods
    and they ground maize, tubers, and seeds on metates into a

nutritious meal for baking into a type of flatbread, and they
stewed and boiled food in willow baskets and ceramic pots.
It required constant time and energy to hunt and butcher, to
gut and skin, to carry, gather, grind, and process their food
and to go out foraging for roots, berries, nuts, and seeds.

The Fremont Indian meal that I ate has taught me to be
more grateful for the hard work of food preparation, and
to make the connection to traditional foods that my own
indigenous ancestors prepared and ate generations ago,
when my Chickasaw and Choctaw great-grandmothers
planted and harvested corn, then ground and milled it
into meal for cornbread, corn fritters, and hominy grits.
They cooked ashela, a Choctaw stew of wild turkey
with vegetables, and they grew pole beans and squash.
They chopped, measured, and mixed in bowls and
cooked and baked in cast-iron skillets and pots over
smokey hearths and hot woodstoves over a century ago.
My mother baked cornbread from scratch and passed
to me the old recipe that her mother had passed to her.
I imagine my great-grandmothers with baskets over their
arms going foraging for roots, berries, nuts, and seeds.

They might think I'm lazy, since it takes me very little
time and effort to prepare food, microwave, or order out.
But, in spring, I plant seeds and grow carrots and herbs
and small tomatoes in garden planters, and in the summer
I buy peaches and melons and squash at farmers' markets.
In early fall, I have a tradition of going to the mountains
to gather chokecherries and elderberries for jams, pinion
nuts for stew, and rose hips for tea, and I leave a note:
"I've gone foraging for roots, berries, nuts, and seeds."

LIVER AND ONIONS

KEITH STEELE

Memoir

I grew up on a small family farm in Southeastern Idaho. Since we had a herd of cattle, we'd have a steer butchered each year. My family had plenty of dinners with hamburger, steaks, or a roast. We also occasionally were served liver and onions. It wasn't a regular meal, but it was a dish with a unique aroma, texture, and taste that I came to enjoy.

In time, I left home and was married. I had a career in the U.S. Air Force, after which I settled in Northern Utah with my wife Janette and our two children. There were occasions through the years when I've had the chance to enjoy a serving of liver and onions. It was maybe only once or twice, but I'd even order them at a restaurant. That was before my surgery. Now, this meal is tied to a worthwhile cause.

EARLY IN 2013, I started getting sick. It wasn't a lingering cough, an unexplained case of the flu, or a typical pain. Instead, I lacked energy and was often tired, but I could never sleep well at night. When I explained the symptoms to my doctor, he would give me a new prescription and say, "It comes with age."

On December 3rd, 2013, however, two coworkers came to me and said, "Keith, you aren't looking good. You need to see a doctor." I told them I had a bad case of middle age and blew them off, explaining that I had an appointment scheduled in a week or so. Soon after that, my boss sat down next to me and echoed my coworkers' concerns. It took me about half an hour before I realized she wasn't taking no for an answer and that I needed medical advice immediately. Fortunately, there was a clinic in the building next to where I worked. The doctor said I had the symptoms of hepatitis.

While waiting at home for the test results to see if I was contagious, my condition went downhill. I developed a distended belly and became jaundiced to the point where even I could see it. On December 13th, 2013 (that was Friday the 13th), my doctor said I wasn't contagious. But he told me to go to the emergency room, where they transported me to a hospital in Salt Lake City. It was my first ride in an ambulance, and they didn't use sirens or even turn on their flashing lights.

In Salt Lake, the doctors told me I had autoimmune hepatitis, which meant my immune system was attacking my liver. My mind was overwhelmed as doctors explained what was happening while I tried to comprehend in days what most sclerosis patients are exposed to over months. Among other things, I learned liver transplants are prioritized based on the score from the model for end-stage liver disease, or MELD score. My score was forty, and I thought that sounded like the middle of the scale. No, that was the top of the scale, defined as gravely ill.

I was dying of liver failure.

One day, a doctor on the transplant team came to my room.

He explained in a somber tone that since my liver wasn't filtering my blood, my kidneys had also stopped functioning. My heart, lungs, and other organs were also shutting down.

I asked him, "You say that I need a transplant. What if it doesn't happen?"

He said, "You have about a week."

My case was unique. Usually, organ failure is caught months or years before surgery is the only option, instead of weeks. I had my wife, two children, and my widowed mother to think about. While I was hoping for the best outcome, I knew I'd already made one decision that would have a positive effect. When I renewed my driver's license in 2010, I checked the box and volunteered to be an organ donor. That choice could change the lives of ten or more people, between tissues and my other organs (except for my liver) that may be usable.

On Saturday, December 21st, the surgeon told me a liver was available, and he was going to travel to inspect it. If it would work for my case, he would transport it back, and I could have the transplant surgery.

"That's great," I said as a cloud of uncertainty started to lift. There was hope that I wouldn't be leaving Janette alone to face life without me.

Several hours later, another member of the transplant team came and told me the surgeon had inspected the liver and would be transporting it back.

I said, "Thank you," and I felt the burden diminish a little more. I wasn't completely out of danger yet, but there was a light at the end of the tunnel.

My surgery started late Saturday night and lasted more than twelve hours. Everything that happened during that time, I've learned from my wife and others.

Janette said she was confident of a successful outcome until late Sunday morning when a doctor called and asked her to come to the surgical floor. She went as requested, leaving our children with a friend. The doctor told her that the transplant had been interrupted because my blood pressure had dropped. They were bringing in experts to correct the problem.

Janette told me that, for the first time, her confidence was overcome with uncertainty and tears. She called her brother, who was able to quickly come to her support. In time, her parents and some friends from church had also gathered to support her.

Before long, my blood pressure stabilized, and the anesthesiologist came out to tell my wife and others, "We almost lost him." The worst part was over, and I was sent to my room in intensive care.

When my surgery started, I expected the next thing I'd see would be Janette telling me all was well. Instead, I was slapped awake by the surgical team. When I asked why, I was told that I'd pulled my breathing tube out, and they didn't want me to damage my vocal cords. My stubborn streak surfaced, and I responded (in a singing voice) with, "Me me me me me me."

I was awake and tired, but the surgery was a success, and my wife was with me. All I could do was lay back while the surgical team made sure my monitors were hooked up right. I was relieved and grateful, but the first chance I had, I asked when I could go home. The nurse informed me that it would be several days at least until they knew I hadn't rejected the transplant. I focused on being a model patient, determined to do the best I could for the sake of my family.

Wednesday was Christmas Day. I spent the morning watching Christmas specials on TV until my family came to visit. It was such a joy to see them for a couple of hours, to be with them and enjoy Christmas as best we could. We opened our presents while I was propped up in my bed. Earlier in the year, we had some family portraits taken. My gift from the family was a few of those pictures in frames to place in my room. But while they were with me, my heart was light, knowing the worst part was behind us.

Janette came to be with me every day to make sure they were taking good care of me. And each night, I'd lay alone in my room, feeling lucky to be alive while trying to not think about how close I'd come to dying. But in my mind, I kept hearing the doctor saying, "You have about a week." I was fortunate that it didn't end that way.

An important part of my recovery was being able to walk. My abdomen had just been sliced open in three directions. At first, I could barely keep my feet under me. Later, as I walked the hospital halls, I would see the portraits of the doctors and the group pictures of the hospital staff. But there was one photograph that looked out of place. I asked the nurse, "What's his story? How come he has his picture here?" I learned his name was Brock, a nephew of one of the doctors on the transplant team. He had liver disease and died at age twenty-one. His story made me feel bad for him and his family. I'm sure he had the same hopes I'd had, and he'd even had the right connections. All I could do is be grateful and make the best of the hand I was dealt.

It doesn't take long to get tired of hospital beds. Shortly after I was able to get up and move around, I was ready to go home. Such was not my luck. The surgery had been a success, but there was still a chance that I'd reject the new liver. I was moved out of intensive care, but at least once, the doctors were concerned that I was rejecting the transplant.

Going home was the beginning of a stressful recovery for Janette. In the middle of winter, I had frequent medical appointments and lab work while getting the kids off to school. Also, per the doctor's orders, I was to stay away from the public. No helping with the shopping, going to the movies, or church. It could have caused a setback if I picked up an illness.

It was almost eight months to the day between when I first

heard that I had hepatitis and when I went back to work. I was elated at first, but I was on a light schedule, and I got tired easily. It was a few more months before I'd recovered enough to work a full day.

I'M STILL REGISTERED as an organ donor. I have two hopes. First, that my story will persuade someone else to volunteer as an organ donor. Second, that someday I can pay it forward. After all, I owe my life to a stranger that was willing to do the same.

It's been about ten years since my surgery. I will always need to take medication to suppress my immune system. I have to get lab work done each quarter and annual exams at the transplant clinic. It has been a bumpy ride, and a couple of times, the doctors were concerned that I was rejecting my new liver. Luckily, they were able to treat me and get things back to my new normal. Each time, whether it's days or months, my chest tightens, and I have to put my faith in the hands of medical experts. For the most part, my life is back to my old routine. I'm able to go out to eat like I used to do. I just can't bring myself to order liver and onions.

SPRING CHICKEN

M.C. ELAINE

Memoir

$\mathcal{N}$inety-eight percent humidity, according to my weather app. I sigh, adjust my Tom Ford sunglasses, and exit from the cranked-up aircon in the mall complex, plunging into the humid soup of an afternoon beyond. I slip my phone into my back jean pocket and adjust my earphones as "Strange Birds" starts playing. I've been stuck on Billie Eilish and Birdy lately and loving every minute of it. The grocery bags rustle. I shift the larger one over to my right hand to balance out the load. Traffic whirrs past on the six-lane stretch of Grange Road leading back to my apartment. I watch the world go by behind the safety of my tinted lenses, transported by the music while following the sidewalk and passing the corner Starbucks. The storefront glass is fogged from the chilled interior, as usual for this time of year in Singapore. The double-decker buses passing by share the same fogged phenomenon.

The bags are heavier than usual. I've decided to take on cooking a whole chicken. It seems about time in my life that I should be able to handle such a task. I'm an adult now. A married woman. And this is what married women do, is it not?

I eye the fresh-pressed orange juice vending machine at the edge of the mall sidewalk, filled with vivid orange fruit. I debate it for a few seconds before giving up on the idea. The grocery bags are too heavy to free up a hand. When I pass out of the mall's shading, the afternoon heat hits full force. Wet season in the tropics blurs with the rest of the year. It's a given that every day will be hot and humid, regardless of season. But days like these are hotter and more humid than most.

My apartment complex soon looms overhead, glass walls glinting. It's not a long walk, maybe ten minutes, but the humidity makes it feel like double that time. I make my way past a handful of construction workers, relieved as always at the fact that unlike in cities such as New York, Miami, and Milan, I've never once had to deal with catcalls. The future MRT station is a noisy site, plastered with worker safety and dengue prevention signs. I consider adjusting the grocery bags to reach my phone and increase the volume. But at this point, I just want to get inside, into the aircon.

I wind through the apartment common grounds—the tennis court, the gym, past the ridiculously large pool I haven't once set toe in, and into the elevator lobby. I elbow the up button and nod my head to the beat of Billie Eilish's "Bad Guy" while waiting. When the elevator comes, it doesn't take long to *ding* at level 9 and open to my apartment entry. I slip off my shoes and pass into the living room. The aircon cascades over my skin, its cool touch heavenly. Our floor-to-ceiling glass windows are fogged on the outside, just like all the mall windows were.

I plop the groceries on the counter and get to work unpacking the mess of double-bagged white plastic. When Reni emerges from the service kitchen, I put on a cheerful smile and remove my earphones. "Good afternoon, Reni," I greet her and bunch up the plastic bags before squeezing them in the spare drawer to use later for bin bags.

"Hi, ma'am," she replies while taking over the unpacking. Her hair is tied up in a ponytail, and her cheeks dimple with a smile before she returns to the fridge with the spring chicken I'd bought as well as an arm full of Yakult, Babybel cheese, almond milk, and miscellaneous items.

I busy myself with putting the pantry items away and escape into the main bedroom. I'm not that much older than Reni, and I doubt I'll ever get used to being called "ma'am." Even after two-plus years, it still always catches me off guard.

When I reemerge into the kitchen and living area, Reni has donned her backpack and is adjusting her hijab by the door. "Done for today, ma'am."

"Ok. Thank you." I ruffle through the cabinets, looking for a spare water bottle. "It's hot out there. Do you need some water?"

"No need, thanks. See you tomorrow," she says with a wave. I close the cabinets and wave back. She disappears into the elevator entry. I wait behind the kitchen counter until the elevator's *ding* and swoosh of doors signal the coast is clear.

My shoulders relax, and I skip over to slump onto the couch and go full-on couch potato, scrolling through my phone and doing absolutely nothing. I message my husband to confirm our dinner time, and after a couple of hours, I switch from social media to search for the chicken recipe I'd wanted to try out. I'm still analyzing the recipe when I pull the chicken from the fridge. I'll have to check it again (and again). My prep time is always double or more what the recipe says it requires, but I'm getting there, step by step.

I slice open the plastic-wrap packaging covering the unassuming bird and pull its slippery body from its final resting place. The glass baking dish waits, the olive oil and sprigs of thyme all on standby. But we have a problem. One that was hidden, tucked under the rib cage for some unfathomable reason. There's a head on this bird. And I ... Don't. Know. What. To. Do.

I put the animal into the baking dish with not-so-mild disgust and stare at it while it stares back at me. I'm an adult, aren't I? I can handle this. I can make the recipe; I just have to ... *remove the head.* I wash my hands, prepare myself with a deep breath, and take hold of a small paring knife.

It doesn't take long for me to give up. I can only stand wrestling with a slimy poultry neck for so long, after all. If the head wants to stay attached, then attached it will stay. Another moment of panic flutters. I check the bird's bottom, praying to not find the innards still in place as well. Relief washes over me when I find a vacant cavity in the place of the fowl's ass. I replace the bird into the dish, surround it with sliced lemon, and rub its slippery skin with olive oil while avoiding looking at its glassy eye. A quick dust with salt and pepper and a handful of thyme later, I happily cover the thing with aluminum foil and place it onto the oven rack.

My husband and I exchange a kiss when he comes home, and I wait until he's left the open-concept living area before rushing to the oven and transporting the finished bird to the service kitchen. It doesn't look half bad ... as long as you look at it from a certain angle. I slice off a generous portion for each plate and arrange a salad next to the crisp-skinned chicken pieces, all while avoiding its dead-eye glare. Once finished plating, I slide the door to the service kitchen closed behind me, plates in hand, and announce that dinner is ready.

"Smells great, babe," my husband assures me while entering the kitchen and grabbing a bottle of wine from the chiller.

"Thanks." I smile to hide my nerves. There's no way I can admit my blunder. I've failed too many times in the kitchen to let him catch on that something is amiss.

He uncorks the Merlot and pours my glass before his. We clink a 'cheers' and dig in. Pride sparks when the white breast hits my tongue. It's moist, well-seasoned, and cooked all the way through. That alone is an achievement for me. My husband acknowledges my progress with a grin. "This is really good."

I nod in agreement and take a big sip of wine. I'll have to do the dishes after this and be confronted by the overcooked chicken head, which, unlike the thicker part of the bird, had not fared so well in the oven.

And it hits me like it does every so often.

I'm not in America anymore.

KIBBLE

VALARIE SCHENK

Poetry

Each day I watch
As Mommy fills
Rover's food dish
Up to the brim.

I think it must
Surely taste good
Since he eats it
With a big grin.

And so when Mom
Is not looking,
I reach down with
My open hand

To pick out a
Few nice morsels
Of firm Kibble—
A fav'rite brand.

I slip them in
My pants pocket
To add to my
Increasing stash,

For which, when I
Have eaten, my
Friend promises
To pay me cash.

At night, after
I'm tucked in bed,
I wait for Mom
To leave my room,

Listen as her
Footsteps quiet,
Slide out of bed
But not too soon.

I pull out my
Bulging shoebox
I keep behind
Soft dangling sheets.

I taste one piece,
Then another,
Liking fully
These nice new treats.

Why haven't I
Tried them sooner?
They are quite good
And taste of flair.

Strange to think I've
Been enlightened
By a childish
And silly dare.

You know this here
Meal's real simple,
Leaving nothing
I have to clean.

I get filled up.
I'm satisfied.
I'm feeling fit,
And still look lean.

So I keep on
Sneaking Kibble
From the supply
Beneath my bed.

And I really
Truly feel fine
'Cept these squirrels
Within my head.

SEAGULLS SAVED THEM AGAIN

KAM HADLEY

Science Fiction

$\mathcal{I}$t was a pioneer relic dating to the 1800s. No one knew what it was used for, but it involved magnets and some type of primitive electricity. Unique and valuable due to its unusual nature, I was proud to have it on display at my historical reenactment museum.

"The first group is gathered and ready to begin the tour," said my manager, William.

"Thank you. I'll be right there." With one last look at the odd machine, I turned and followed William to the front of the museum.

The crowd was moving about with excitement, but they quieted as I pinned a roving microphone to my chest and addressed the group.

"Welcome to this unique Utah historical reenactment museum. My name is Collette. We have put together a collection for you that you won't see anywhere else in the world. Welcome to the Pioneer Experience."

The day passed in a blur. I introduced each group and

oversaw things in general, running around and putting out the proverbial fires. Finally, the last group, reserved for family, assembled in the lobby. The stragglers from the group before still loitered around the mysterious machine, but that was natural.

I passed around a plate of cookies I had made from an authentic pioneer recipe. I admired the way the pioneers made use of all their resources. Collecting the seagull poop was an experience I would never forget, but somehow it was fine in the cookies.

With the family group munching, I checked on the stragglers. The kids were a little rambunctious for a museum setting, but the parents were trying to take pictures. Hopefully, they would be done soon.

Returning to the family group, I was shocked to see my cousin, Leisha, pouring ketchup over her cookies. Flames ignited inside me. The pioneers didn't have ketchup! Wait. Did they? I suppose they could've, but I doubted they ate it on their cookies.

Leisha smiled smugly from behind her plate, enjoying every bite. Snatching the bottle, I went to hide it before anyone else could get ahold of it when a forceful blast of light knocked us off our feet. Children screamed, but we lay on the ground, unable to gather our senses.

When I opened my eyes, a haze hung in the air. My body ached as if I'd lain there for hours. Around me, people roused, rubbing their eyes. Sending William for bandages, I assessed people personally. Leisha was there too. She had an ability to cheer people and lighten the moment.

Bumps and bruises were all the injuries anyone had. I breathed a sigh of relief. Responsibility bore down on me, but the weight lifted with the reassurance that everyone was well.

The blast had come from the direction of the mysterious machine. As I approached, one of the children started babbling.

"I'm so sorry. I didn't mean to. I didn't know that it would do anything."

"What did you do?" The child's father demanded.

"I wasn't the only one. Sammy was pushing buttons too. I stepped on this pedal thing and pulled a lever like I was driving."

"We're very sorry," the mother began apologizing.

Her act of contrition was interrupted by sirens. A police bullhorn ordered us all to remain where we were as the site was secured.

A patrol unit in hazmat suits took an annoying amount of time going over everything. Really, wasn't that a bit overkill? We were all fine. Nobody was hurt. Who even called them?

After an eternity of waiting, William and I were invited to meet with the squad leader.

"I am Officer Rivera," a man said stiffly, not removing even the hood of his hazmat suit. "A contaminant was released from this site today with a force that instantly caused the deaths of hundreds of people in the neighboring towns. How you are all alive is a mystery. You and all of the people here are required to remain on site until further notice."

"Well, at least we have cookies." I tried to lighten the mood.

"And ketchup," Leisha added, poking around the corner.

I nodded. If ketchup distracted people and brought them any amount of joy in this situation, then by all means, let them eat their cookies with ketchup.

Three days passed in tedium. The cookies had all been eaten. A supply truck delivered necessary items for us to get by. Leisha was invaluable during this time, keeping up morale and giving us something to laugh about, but sleeping on the floor was getting old.

Eventually, a medical team wearing hazmat suits came and did a health check on all of us, finding us well. Five hundred people in the surrounding area were dead, but the museum tourists were alive and healthy. It was determined that the blast had emanated from the mysterious machine, which had been confiscated. Grudgingly, we were allowed to return to our homes on the condition we remain available for immediate contact.

Mormon Superweapon Kills Hundreds, read headlines, both nationally and internationally. Yes, we made international news. Reporters came from far and wide seeking interviews. A few tourists shared their experiences, but I refused comment. That is until Officer Rivera showed up on my porch.

I didn't recognize him out of his hazmat suit, but he showed his badge and edged his way inside with a stern manner. Flanking him were two other officers whom he did not introduce. I let them inside, but none of us sat down.

"Ms. Alvord," Rivera intoned, "I will cut to the chase. All of the people that lived through the blast from the superweapon had something in common. Every one of them had eaten cookies that day. Cookies you made."

"My pioneer cookies?" The question hung in the air until I laughed. The look on Rivera's face made me laugh harder.

"Ms. Alvord. This is not something to laugh about. I need that recipe."

Rivera followed me to the kitchen, where I retrieved my photocopy of the pioneer cookie recipe. Rivera read aloud, "2 Cups Flour, ½ teaspoon Salt, 1/3 Cup Molasses, 1 Cup Seagull Droppings …" He trailed off. "What? Seagull Droppings? As in, poop? Surely you didn't." He looked at me.

I nodded. "The cookies needed to be authentic. I spent the day on Antelope Island, and let me tell you, gathering enough droppings was no easy trick."

Rivera's eyes were wide, aghast.

"Well, I did discover that if I startled them just right, they would usually leave me a nice sample."

Rivera shook his head and massaged his temples. "Seagull

poop, seagull poop," he muttered. Then, he and his goons left my house, taking my recipe without even asking.

"The gall of them," I proclaimed to myself. "Incredibly rude."

But that night, the recipe hit the news. *Pioneer recipe containing seagull poop saved the lives of over a hundred people in Utah. A mysterious blast last Saturday killed over five hundred, yet these folks survived.* Turning up the volume, I listened to more of the story.

Mormon pioneers said seagulls saved them. Now we know the gulls saved them in more than one way.

Another voice took up the historical account. "Summer 1848, crickets swarmed the Salt Lake Valley, threatening to destroy crops and fields. Seagulls miraculously came to the rescue, eating up crickets and saving the Mormons."

The first reporter came back on. "Mormon pioneers went on to create a superweapon, the details of which are still largely unknown. Early saints did have enemies." Depictions of Johnston's Army were shown onscreen as the reporter continued, "Though the weapon appears previously unused, one thing is certain. The seagulls have saved them again."

Huh. I rested my chin on my fist. Who would've thought?

My comfort food is russian borscht. What's yours? Inna V Lyon

FROM RUSSIA WITH BORSCHT

INNA V. LYON

Memoir

Inna

J check my watch for the tenth time—three hours and fifteen minutes before boarding. The impending departure time is approaching fast. The moment Seryozha and I step over that line at the security checkpoint of the Sheremetyevo International Airport, our lives will change forever. Shudders run through my body. I clench and unclench my fists a few times. Spending a month in a hospital where they patched my stomach after a case of internal bleeding hadn't helped my nerves to settle down.

"Inna, are you listening?" my mother asks me.

"What? What did you ask?"

"Will you give me a call when both of you arrive in Salt Lake City?"

"Yes, of course I will. As soon as I find out if they have a landline or cell phone, figure out the time difference with

Russia, the long-distance call rates, and how long I can be on the phone."

Mom tries to smile but wipes her eyes instead.

Russian superstitions say that on the first part of a trip, you think about what is left behind, and during the second part, what lies ahead. March 26th, 2003, proves them wrong. All I can think about is how to get us—my eleven-year-old son and I— to our new home in Salt Lake City, Utah, in the United States. I would worry about what I left behind later.

I have never been anywhere outside of Russia, and I have no idea how to get around Sheremetyevo, the biggest airport I've ever seen—to say nothing of the looming challenge of JFK. I stutter every time I open my mouth and speak English to someone. I have no experience going through security or talking to the border patrol officers. My catchphrase, "Please, speak slowly," might not get me far. All I have with me is a Russian-English pocket dictionary, a folder thick with paperwork, a few dollar bills, and U.S. visas in our passports. Our simple belongings fit into a huge colorful suitcase that my son will be lugging around; as a result of surgery, I have lifting restrictions. And I hope that, somehow, we will find family, friends, and a home in a faraway land.

"Inna, dear, we will see each other again." My sister squeezes my hand in hers.

I nod. Tears in my throat, I squawk, "Yes," not believing that it will ever happen. I don't have the luxury of crying in front of my mom. The determination in her eyes to tear our airline tickets to pieces, canceling the international marriage on the spot, is too obvious.

"Mom, it's been fifteen minutes. We need to go." Seryozha comes back from exploring the nearby shops. He acts just like a kid too excited to be on a plane for the first time.

Trying to hide my jitters, I get up. All goodbyes are spoken. All hugs are given multiple times. No more borrowed minutes being with my loved ones. I grab Seryozha's hand in mine, my carry-on bag in another, and take my first step into a new life.

THE EIGHT-HOUR FLIGHT from Moscow to New York feels like forever.

The newspapers passed around by the flight attendants are still in Russian. So are the movies in our personal consoles in front of us. But everything else is so foreign, and I don't understand half of what people around me are saying. I want to hide inside my heavy fur coat's hood and sob for a few minutes, but Seryozha is too excited to miss even a minute of our new adventures. He turns to me. "I almost peed my pants when the plane took off. Mom, are we going to fly over the ocean? Just imagine if the plane breaks—we will be swimming in the cold water."

I'd rather not imagine that, or I, too, will pee my pants.

Seryozha presses the button to call a flight attendant.

"Can I have tomato juice?" he asks. The flight attendant smiles and brings him two boxes of juice.

We eat something, ordering some food using our best English. We stand in line for the airplane bathroom. Seryozha begs me for money and buys something from the catalog of useless merchandise. Spoken English is deafening to me. Mom, why didn't you tear up our tickets? Will I ever again feel the warmth of your embrace and hear familiar Russian speech?

Getting through the U.S. border is humiliating. Despite our rigorous English lessons, the customs control officer can't understand us. She calls for an interpreter's help over the phone.

"Czy rozumiesz język polski?"

The Polish interpreter has enough vocabulary to understand

27

that even though I'm already the wife of a U.S. citizen, we are coming on a fiancé visa. The process takes over forty minutes before we hear the hackneyed phrase, "Welcome to America," with the desirable thud of a stamp in our passports.

The JFK airport overwhelms us with its size, colors, and indifference to its two small, tired Russian passengers. Unknown smells, multinational crowds, signs, flashy billboards, and mumbled announcements—all in English, too fast to read or understand. Too big. Too noisy. Too unfamiliar.

"Mom, I want to buy something. I want to do it myself."

Seryozha makes it a goal to spend our last twenty-dollar bill on food and drinks. A bottle of Coke and a box of cookies takes it all. Converted into Russian rubles, that twenty would've bought us our weekly groceries.

The five-hour layover in JFK, and the following four-and-a-half-hour flight to Salt Lake City, drains the last of our energy. It is nighttime in Russia, and we zone out as soon as we find our seats on the back of the airplane to Salt Lake. No drink or snack offer could keep us awake.

Upon arrival to Salt Lake, I think about how we need to go through another customs embarrassment and keep looking around. But, thankfully, no mean border watchdogs, fast-English questions, or quick fingers going through our paperwork bother us. We keep moving along with other passengers.

"Mom, how much longer?"

I have the same question. All we want is to lie down and close our eyes for a good ten hours.

My bag gets heavier with every step. Seryozha checks on me often, but day-long exhaustion takes over my son. He falls to his knees in the middle of the airport's hallway. I help him up to his feet, thankful for the carpeted floor. Even Moscow's fanciest international airport has only tiled floors. America keeps blowing my mind with its weird customs and huge, oversized spaces.

A welcoming hug from my American husband Paul and his youngest daughter Laila relieves me of the duty of getting us overseas. We have made it. We are here. America is our new home. So why do my tears taste bitter?

Laila

THE AIRPORT NEVER SLEEPS, thought Laila. Then she yawned, tucked her arm under Dad's, and leaned into his shoulder. After the Winter Olympics last year, this place got even busier with new routes and an increased number of visitors. The never-ending stream of busy people in the Salt Lake City International Airport waiting area kept moving down the escalator to the luggage carousels and the exit doors for ground transportation.

Laila and Dad stood in front of the escalator to get a better view of the gates admitting the newly arrived passengers.

The flight from New York had been delayed twice, and Laila had passed her bedtime a long time ago. Late or not, Laila wouldn't miss going to the airport for anything. They were arriving today—Dad's new wife and her eleven-year-old son, the same age as Laila. They had flown all the way from Russia, and Laila would be the first among her siblings to meet the new family members.

"Delta flight DL845 New York to Salt Lake City has landed. The luggage carousel is number 3."

At last, Laila would see her new stepmom and stepbrother. They looked nice in the pictures, but in videos, both had a heavy European accent, rolled their hard R's, and forgot articles when they spoke.

Mom and Dad divorced three years prior. Laila was too little to remember how it had been before when Mom preferred Dad travel less and stay home more. A legal separation and ugly divorce were in the past, but her parents' continuing hard feelings toward each other made it difficult to feel happy family vibes.

Laila loved them both, but having four siblings divided her parents' time unequally, favoring the youngest. Laila was the youngest and spent time playing house with her siblings, cuddling with Mom, and being spoiled by Dad. She was a happy kid with big blue eyes and even bigger glasses in heavy frames. Things changed when Dad moved out. A counselor appointed Laila visitation time with Dad every other weekend. That was three years ago. Lately, Mom has been busy with her new real estate career and often lets Laila visit her dad after school during the week.

Last year, Dad broke the news he was getting married again. Her oldest siblings had already speculated that he traveled to Europe too often, and they were right. He'd visited Russia eight times within two years, once spending over a month there. Now his new wife Inna and her son Sergey were arriving in Utah.

More passengers slipped through the exit gates. Laila left the warmth of her dad's shoulder, took a couple of steps toward the gates, and tried to pick their party out from the crowd.

They would look different, those Russians, she thought.

A tall black fur hat with three bushy tails showed up in the river of passengers' heads for a second, then disappeared. That was a funny hat. Laila fixed her blue beret with the 2002 Olympic Games logo more securely on her own head. Dad volunteered at the Games, and she got perks and merchandise. This blue beret was her favorite.

A minute later, the funny fur hat surfaced again. This time it was attached to a heavy brown fur coat. Inside the coat was a tired woman with a pale face clutching a black bag with one hand and a skinny boy's hand with the other. They moved slowly, missing the beat of the hastily moving crowd.

"That's them," said Dad. He moved toward the woman with open arms. "Inna, Sergey, welcome to the U.S."

The boy ran to hug Dad, and the woman smiled and stopped, losing her grip on her bag.

Inna

THE FIRST COUPLE of days after our arrival in Utah, all we want to do is sleep.

In the morning, Seryozha and I put on brave faces, but by noon, fatigue takes over, and we both crawl back to our beds.

At the end of our second day, my husband's sister, now my sister-in-law, brings us two dishes—chicken and rice casserole and apple pie. I find them plain and boring, but she tells me to keep the fancy blue glass dishes as a welcoming present.

On the third day, my son and I break into hives from the change in climate, unfamiliar food, and water. The cortisone cream offered by my husband Paul helps with the itch but makes us sleepier. "You have to stay awake," says my husband. "It is called *jet lag,* and it will go away when you adjust to American time."

Easy for him to say. We'd never flown that far nor experienced so many time zone changes.

Seryozha thinks that jet lag translates into "airplane feet," and so we shake our feet as often as we can the next day. It helps, and each morning, our curiosity about the new country takes over, and we brave the daylight.

On Friday, my husband takes us to our first American restaurant—Hometown Buffet. The variety of food to choose from blows my mind—Chinese, Italian, Mexican, a salad bar, roast beef, all kinds of fish, bread, and even beef liver with onions, desserts, and ice cream stations.

My husband is eating tacos. Seryozha's plate has mountains of mashed potatoes on it. I have a bit of everything that looks exotic. To my disappointment, the food doesn't taste as good as it looks. It is missing something. It has enough seasoning, fat, and sweetness, but it lacks real taste. I don't know exactly what's wrong with it, but even after I'm full, I don't feel satisfied.

I'm a foodie. I'm a cook. I think that a country and culture are best learned through their cuisine. American food tastes like cardboard.

I see my husband's worried look, eyeing my untouched plate. I love him for his worry, kindness, dedication, and concern.

I don't like America, and I don't like its food.

Laila

LAILA COULDN'T WAIT until her next visit to Dad's. Friday, right after school, Mom dropped her off at Dad's house on Pioneer Road, and Laila ran inside, forgetting to kiss Mom goodbye.

"See ya!" Laila remembered to yell and burst through the front door.

Dad and Inna greeted her in the kitchen. Inna didn't look sleepy anymore. She wore black dress pants, a blue sweater with rhinestones adorning the collar, a silk scarf around her neck, full makeup, and her hair done.

"Are you guys going on a date?" asked Laila.

"No," replied Inna. "I'm getting ready to cook dinner."

Laila didn't know that to cook dinner, a woman must dress nicely and apply makeup. Maybe it was a Russian thing.

"What are you going to cook?"

"Potatoes with chicken." Inna turned to Dad. "Or I need to say—chicken and potatoes?"

"Either way is okay," said Dad.

"Where is Sergey?" asked Laila. She wanted to talk to him. He will be going to school with her next week.

Dad replied, "He is playing video games in the living room. Do you want to join him?"

Laila hesitated. "Only if you come with me."

Dad nodded, hugged Inna, and followed Laila to the living room. Sergey occupied one of the banana chairs and played a racing game, sometimes yelling in Russian, "Ah ti sobaka!"

Dad waved at him to stop and explained to Sergey that all three of them would play together, taking turns with the two available controllers.

Laila knew that Dad was a patient man but was amazed again at how calm and gentle Dad was as he explained the game's rules, acronyms, characters, and lingo to Sergey.

The cutthroat concept was hard to explain, but when Dad mentioned "win-lose," Sergey nodded.

Time flew by. A couple of hours later, Inna called them to the kitchen for dinner.

Placemats, pink napkins, shining cutlery, and a little vase with a pine branch waited for them. A blue ceramic casserole dish with a steaming entree sat in the middle of the table. A plate with bread, a butter dish, and a jar of mayo were also served. The food smelled delicious.

Laila didn't ask any questions and watched Inna serve everyone a generous pile of hot potatoes with chicken. Laila wouldn't have minded having a salad first, but she didn't see any greens.

After the blessing, everyone dug into their food.

Inna and Sergey passed the mayo jar to each other and applied a generous portion on top of their food. Yuck! Laila's older sister, Marie, hated mayo and constantly reminded everyone how unhealthy it was. Laila didn't like it either. Apparently, Inna and Sergey never read food labels or worried about saturated fats in their diet. They buttered their bread, and Sergey added another spoonful of mayo to his plate.

Laila took a piece of potato, blew on it, and took a bite. It was good. A bit salty to Laila's taste, but juicy and tasty. Next, she picked up the chicken. She took one bite, tasted something slimy, and spat it in her napkin.

"What?" asked Inna with genuine concern in her voice.

"Chicken fat. I tasted it. You probably forgot to trim this piece."

"Fat? Trim the fat? Do you mean—cut off the chicken fat? We never do that. It is the best part. That is what makes food taste—fat."

Laila felt her stomach stick in her throat. Her sister Marie's healthy talks and disgust for anything fattening was deeply engraved into their household cooking. Mom always trimmed the fat from anything they ate. She might burn pizzas, bread, and cookies, but she didn't forget to trim the chicken fat—ever.

Laila took a couple more bites of potato but couldn't make herself finish the food on her plate. The yucky, slimy taste of chicken fat was on her mind until everyone finished their meal.

For dessert, they warmed up apple pie her aunt Sylva brought yesterday.

Thank goodness for American desserts. Laila felt safe eating something prepared by her American relatives.

After dinner, Dad taught Inna that she didn't have to wash the dishes by hand; that's what the dishwasher was for. Inna wrote down the meaning of the buttons in her blue notebook.

Laila sighed. It would be a long time before they could have a full conversation or for Inna to be able to answer Laila's questions.

Over the next two months, Laila witnessed many of Inna's and Sergey's nuisances, adjusting to their new life.

Inna's notes about the dishwasher failed to explain that nothing except dishwasher detergent could be used for the machine. Apparently, washing detergent was the same thing for them. She washed the house floor for a couple of hours.

Sergey warmed up a baked potato, still wrapped in aluminum foil, in the microwave, causing a small explosion that cost Dad a new microwave, along with the pleasure of installing it himself.

Inna found American desserts too sweet but failed when she tried to bake her signature honey cake. Dad told Laila that Inna had tossed her hard-as-a-rock cake in the garbage.

She baked another cake from a box and used raw eggs whipped with sugar instead of cake frosting. That beautifully decorated cake was given to the neighbors who, rumor had it, took a bunch of pictures and didn't eat it, fearing Salmonella contamination.

Sergey hated all American cheese, complaining that it tasted like sawdust.

At the family party, Laila's Uncle Lowell forced Inna to try a bloody hamburger, and Inna screamed after taking the first bite, seeing blood dripping onto her plate. Uncle Lowell killed Inna's craving for classic American meals forever.

Later, Dad told Laila that Inna refused to eat hamburgers anywhere and ate just hamburger buns as bread with any meal.

The school year was almost over. Sergey stayed after school to learn English with a tutor. He also had a Walkman cassette player to listen to books in English. He loved it and carried it everywhere, explaining to everyone that "he was doing his homework." His language improved significantly in just two months.

Inna also went to school—the English as a Second Language school—but she complained that it was too far away and would go only when Dad had time to drive her there. She read the Russian detective series she brought with her and watched YouTube videos in Russian on Sergey's computer.

Every dinner at Dad's house was a culinary adventure, and Laila watched like a hawk for dangerous ingredients on her plate. The untrimmed chicken dinner was too hard to forget. She made sure she had a stash of cookies and candies in her backpack whenever she visited Dad's house.

One day Dad took Inna and Sergey to see the new movie "Brother Bear." It wasn't Laila's week to visit, and she was a bit upset that they didn't wait for her.

When Laila arrived, Inna offered her a peanut butter sandwich as an after-school snack. Laila refused, not knowing how to explain to Inna without offending her cooking skills that she liked her sandwich without bread crust.

Inna chatted about visiting Hometown Buffet for lunch and the movie theater afterward with Dad and Sergey. Both places surprised her. In her broken English, she tried to explain the variety of meals at the buffet and the story plot about the little bear named Kenai. It was a circus and pantomime show combined. Inna didn't have enough vocabulary to retell the plot of the little bear adventure. She gesticulated, jumped, ran around the table, and howled about the movie scenes.

"And Kenai goes like this," Inna said, climbing on the chair, imitating the bear going through the mountains.

"And his brother Sitka goes like this," she said, dropping on the floor, reenacting the bear dying.

"And Kenai goes like this," she said, sitting on the carpet, rubbing her eyes, and pretending to cry.

It was very entertaining, but Laila didn't get any of it. She made a mental note to go see that movie with her mom and siblings. At least Inna tried to have a full conversation with her. Well, a one-sided conversation.

Inna

A WEEK AFTER OUR ARRIVAL, the first week of April, my husband took me to ESL, the English as a Second Language class. I passed the placement test and joined the mid-level group. I studied grammar and conversation. It turned out that my English was not so bad. In ESL school, there were many people from Mexico and Brazil; they kept to themselves. There was no one else from Russia. I was alone. The school was boring, unfamiliar, and complicated. I can't say I enjoyed it.

Now it is summer break at ESL, and I'm in a different school —A-1 driving school—along with a bunch of 15-year-old teenagers. They already know how to drive. After walking to the post office in 104-degree heat, I know I want to learn how to drive.

My husband comes back from a business trip to Washington. I'm fascinated that there are two of them—Washington State and the capital, Washington D.C. I didn't know that.

My husband invites all four of us to visit Larissa, his Russian tutor, who has given him a few language lessons in the past. Larissa moved to the US from Russia about ten years ago. She works as a clerk at a retail store and occasionally gives Russian lessons. My husband's vocabulary of four words—"love, husband, pillow, and blanket"— make me doubt Larissa's tutoring skills.

Larissa lives in a fancy downtown apartment with access to a gym and a swimming pool. We meet her in the lobby. Light green capris and a white T-shirt fit her petite figure like a glove. She is blonde and chatty. I feel a pang of jealousy when Larissa and my husband hug each other. I still can't understand this American greeting. In Russia, you only hug people you know well. Do they know each other well? I will find out later. For now, I hang on each word and try to convince myself I'm not jealous.

"Inna, you came to America in March, right?" asks Larissa. "How do you like it here?" She speaks English with a heavy Russian accent. Do I speak like that, too?

"It's fine," I lie.

On our way here, my husband called Larissa's apartment a 'little Russia,' and now I see why. Her two-bedroom apartment looks like any Russian home: Russian books on the shelves,

Russian nesting dolls lining the table, and wall posters with Alla Pugacheva, a Russian singer. Larissa turns down the blaring TV playing a movie in (of course) Russian and points to her couch.

"Sit."

Russians are very hospitable, and I expect some food to be served to us guests. Larissa offers only pistachio ice cream. Seryozha and I love it. I need to find out where she buys it.

"I go buy ice cream at Albertsons. It is really good and yumm. I add more pee-staa-chio," says Larissa, answering my thoughts. "I think they ... what the word ... oh, greedy when they do not put more nuts."

Larissa speaks English with a heavy accent and misses her articles. I realize that is how I speak. After three months in America, Seryozha's English is much better than both of us combined. My son has a knack for languages. Video games with his friends certainly helps. Sonic and Zelda rule.

A few minutes later, Larissa's daughter shows up. Larissa's carbon copy has the same name—Larissa. But college student Larissa has much better English than her mother and much worse manners. She greets us, gives us a lopsided smile, and slams the door to her bedroom. I get the vibe that the daughter does not approve of her mother inviting Russian friends over. I want to know their story.

We take turns changing into bathing suits in a tiny bathroom and go to the indoor community pool.

"Mom, Laila, watch me diving!" yells Seryozha before anyone can warn him of the sign on the wall: "No diving." Too late. Splash. Boom. Seryozha cannonballs into the middle of the pool, sending a wave of cold water over the rest of our party. I laugh looking at our wet company.

"Eww, I'm wet," complains Laila.

"Well, you'll get wet eventually if you are getting in the water," reasons my husband.

The water is fresh and pleasant. Larissa and my husband

chat in the lounge chairs. Seryozha wants to do it all—noodle fighting, Marco Polo, and pretending he is a walrus, slipping off the pool's edge into the water, making it look like a not-too-splashy cannonball.

I like the pool, but I want to leave and take my husband away from Larissa, who pats his hand too casually.

On our way home, the car air smells like chemicals. Larissa told us to take our showers at home. She didn't have towels for all of us. Seryozha plays on his Gameboy, and Laila listens to her iPod.

"Did you like Larissa?" asks my husband.

"I like ice cream," I answer too fast.

What is going on? Am I jealous? I sigh.

"She is fine. How many times did she give you Russian lessons?" The question has been on my mind since morning when my husband announced our visit downtown.

"Only a couple of times. I traveled too much to have more lessons. Then I figured out that you needed English more than I need Russian."

I nod. It is a good thing that he only had two lessons. Why did they hug?

My husband continues, "I don't want you to turn out like Larissa."

"What do you mean? She seems fine to me. She has a fancy apartment, a job, pistachio ice cream, and a rude daughter."

I hope I will never have to visit her again. My husband doesn't need more Russian lessons. I can teach him all the Russian he wants.

My husband clarifies, "I don't want you to be like Larissa, stuck between two countries."

"Do you want me to forget my motherland?"

"Not forget. But to give America a chance. To embrace a new culture and perfect your use of the language, you must immerse yourself into your new life. If you keep watching Russian TV, surrounding yourself with Russian trinkets and books, you won't have time to learn new customs and speak good English."

"I went to ESL school for two months to study English."

"Yes. But you speak Russian to Sergey, and you don't have any friends outside the family because you can't carry a good conversation in English."

"It's unfair. I speak English."

"Not enough to get around without me."

I sniffle. I'm on the edge of tears, but I feel that this conversation is important, and I hold back.

"Inna, darling, listen," he says. "I'm not telling you to leave your old life and country behind and never speak of it again. I'm asking you to give the US a chance. Try to learn more about everything around you, to speak, read, and write in English. Your Russian roots will always be with you, but today is your opportunity to accept the life you chose when we got married."

I sniffle again.

"You saw Larissa. She's made her home a shrine to Russia. She watches Russian TV and listens to Russian radio. She speaks Russian to her daughter and has poor grammar, even after ten years in the States. She couldn't find a decent job except as a store clerk because of her limited conversation skills. But her daughter is already making all the right choices—going to college, hanging out with native speakers, reading, and studying in English."

"I'm not as young as Seryozha or Larissa's daughter."

"Inna, my dear wife, you are capable of doing anything you want. Just make it your goal. I will help you. I'm always here for you, but I'll be traveling again for business, and you will need to go around by yourself—drive to college, meet different people, and eventually find a job. You can do it. You are brave and smart. Don't give up."

I search for the tissues in my purse, but the hot tears don't wait for me to find a soft Aloe Vera case.

THERE IS no manual at the library for how to become an American.

But that Saturday visit to Larissa's swimming pool changed my degree of perseverance and my daily routine.

I start calling my son by his full name, Sergey. Seryozha is too tongue-twisting for Americans. His short name is too private and dear to me. I reserve it for our rare conversations in Russian.

I passed the driving test. Now, when my husband travels, I drive with Sergey to Albertson's to get pistachio ice cream and to the library to get books in English for Sergey. I get my first English book, *The Day No Pigs Would Die*, by R.N. Peck. I read the book every day, keeping the dictionary next to me and writing all the unknown words into a notebook. It is a slow process.

I don't watch Russian channels or Russian YouTube videos anymore.

I speak English to Sergey, go to church, or take piano lessons from a neighbor— all in English, expanding my vocabulary and circle of friends. Church activity opens a new realm for me— from canning to scrapbooking, the hobby opportunities are endless.

The new school year starts in the middle of August. It is so weird; all schools and colleges in Russia start on September 1st. I load my textbooks into a bag with my husband's company's logo and drive the old-fashioned Chevrolet Cutlass to the train station. The ESL school is on 3300 South, and it takes me forty minutes by train and another twenty minutes by bus to get there. I go there every day, and I'm in the advanced class now.

Sergey is excited about middle school and taking a school bus. His English is really good, and he corrects my pronunciation and word choice. He grasps the language through games with his friends from school, the neighborhood, and youth activities. He reads all the available Harry Potter books over and over. He gets a beaten-up skateboard from a friend and practices outside for hours. Looking at his new summer spiky haircut and AC/DC T-shirt, sun-tanned face, and scraped knees, I would have never guessed this boy had lived anywhere else but America.

The food is another story. My Russian culinary degree in public catering and years of working in restaurants seem to fail every time I try to cook something unfamiliar.

When my husband asks me about the food, I want to explain to him how Russian produce is "full of taste," grown without chemicals and pesticides, and always fresh from local markets. But I don't have enough vocabulary to do it yet, so I simply say, "It is not yummy."

He traveled the world and tried so many different cuisines and meals. But he is a die-hard American and loves everything about it, including tasteless, salty fast food.

My husband's oldest daughter Janette gives me a four-quart crock pot. For the next two weeks, our house smells like beef stew or chicken noodle soup, depending on the day of the week.

I try recipes from Japanese and Mexican cuisines. I can't say I've mastered them. Some turn out successful, and some—well, not edible.

On Labor Day weekend, Sergey leaves for Idaho for a couple of days with his friend to ride four-wheelers and go fishing. My husband Paul is returning from his business trip to Seattle. I wake up alone and realize that I don't want to do anything. I don't even want to drive to get pistachio ice cream. I don't want to finish my book *The Day No Pigs Would Die*. I don't want to change from my pajamas or put on makeup.

Suddenly, I'm so homesick in this big empty house and would give anything to be back in my tiny room with a common bathroom in the hostel where I lived with Sergey for the last six years. There, I spoke, sang, read, and cracked jokes in Russian. I cooked Russian food and didn't know how blessed I had been there, in humble circumstances and modest living, having friends and delicious meals. I miss everything. I miss my family, my mom, my sister, and friends. And I miss the food.

I want to call my mom, but I exceeded the money limit on my Noble phone card. I can send an email, but I decide to lie down and cry. Will America ever feel like home?

Laila

DAD RETURNED from Seattle Saturday morning and called the home number, asking Laila if she could go shopping with him.

"Shopping for me?" asked Laila.

"A little bit for you, and a little bit for Inna. I need your advice on what to get her. She is in a sour mood and won't tell me why."

"Ok, we can go. I know what to get her. She asked me recently about scrapbooking supplies and where to get them. We can try that new Michaels store on 12600 South."

Dad picked up Laila and told her that when he returned from his trip, he'd found Inna in her pajamas with red puffy eyes, still in bed at noon. She didn't get out of bed and wouldn't tell him what was wrong. The only thing he could find out was that nothing hurt, and no one had died. Sergey was with his friend's family for a short trip to Idaho and wouldn't return for another day.

"I think she misses home," added Dad at the end of his story.

Laila nodded. On her last visit, she found a pile of untouched library books in English. She couldn't imagine not seeing her mom and family for as long as Inna had.

Laila and Dad stopped at Ross to get Laila a new lime-green

and yellow T-shirt. Michaels was the next stop. With the store clerk's advice, they bought a scrapbooking album, glue sticks, a set of paper, and stickers.

"She will love it," Laila assured Dad.

At 3:15 p.m., Inna was still in her pajamas but had left her bed and now sat in the corner on the floor behind the dresser. They could only see the back of her head—her hair a mess—but not her face because she was rolled into a ball, face-down on the carpet.

"Hi, sweetheart. See what Laila and I got you," said Dad, placing two Michaels bags on top of the dresser.

"What is it?" asked a hoarse voice from the corner.

"Scrapbooking supplies. I hope you'll like it. It's for creating pages of happy memories. You take pictures ..."

A long howl from the corner interrupted Dad's explanations.

"I don't have any happy memories," cried Inna. "I have no friends. I spent this summer alone, reading stupid English books with no sense. I miss my mom, and I want to go back to Russia."

Dad and Laila sat on the floor next to Inna, curled up in her pink pajamas. Dad took Inna's hand in his. She pulled it back. He put his hand on her shoulder. His soft voice always consoled Laila when she had a scraped knee or got in a quarrel with her older sisters. She only hoped that he would find the right words for Inna, too. If Inna went back, Dad would be so sad. Sergey wouldn't want to go back. He'd told her about a horrible, small apartment with no bathroom where they'd lived in Russia. Laila didn't want them to go back.

Dad's gentle voice carried over. "Inna, darling. Being nostalgic is okay. You lived there for thirty-five years, and you've been in America only for six months. There will be times when we'll go to Russia and visit your family. And they will come here to visit America, too."

Inna grabbed Dad's hand. He continued.

"We love you and Sergey. You are both part of our family now. I want you to be happy and have a happy life here with us, with me. Please, don't cry. You will have friends because you have a good heart, and you are a very sociable person. Just give it time."

The pink ball sniffled.

"But I miss my home and Russian stuff."

"Stuff like what?" asked Dad.

"Like my mom, aunt, sister, cats, and food."

Dad looked at Laila. Laila read the question in his eyes. Cats?

"Well, I can't bring any of your family members here right away. But we can talk with the landlord about having a cat. But for food—you are the best cook. You can cook your Russian food anytime you want. There is a Russian store on 4500 South. We can go there and buy some Russian produce, and you can cook whatever you want. We call that 'comfort food.' Why don't we try that?"

The pink ball uncurled, and Inna's puffy face appeared from beneath her shaggy hair.

"Russian store? Why didn't you tell me before? I can cook Russian food? And you won't be mad?"

Dad shrugged his shoulders, looked at Laila, and smiled.

"Why would I be mad?"

"Well, you said you don't want our home to look like Larissa's little Russia."

"You can cook your Russian food anytime you want. I'm sure everyone will love it."

THE HOUSE SMELLED OF FOOD. Not any food Laila had tried before, but something so sweet and, at the same time, spicy. It smelled like some kind of mix of boiled vegetables, with garlic prevailing over the scent of cabbage and carrots.

"Wash your hands," Inna told her. "I prepared my favorite Russian food called Borscht, and I want you to try it too. It took me three hours to cook it," she explained. "And I cut off all the fat from the chicken."

Laila left her backpack and jacket and washed her hands in the bathroom sink. Returning to the kitchen, she sat down at the table.

"What about Sergey?" she asked.

"He will eat later. Bryce and Chase were waiting for him. Boys' stuff. I waited to share this meal with you," replied Inna.

After a blessing on the food, Inna placed a white bowl of red soup in front of Laila.

The large bowl holding steamy red soup stood on the table, accompanied by a white napkin and spoon. It smelled of something so unique and different that Laila couldn't place it first. Tomato sauce? Boiled potatoes? Cooked chicken?

Tiny specks of crushed garlic and fresh, chopped dill adorned the top of the soup. Laila took her spoon and scooped her first spoonful of Inna's soup. The hot liquid filled her mouth.

All at once, Inna's personality burst out of that bowl of red soup. All of her scrupulousness and generosity. Her desire to blend her culture, family, and country, and her desire to keep her ethnicity and individuality. Her spontaneity and gustiness, her inquisitiveness, restlessness, creativity, uniqueness, loneliness, and homesickness for a land and country she would never fully be part of again.

The plate of hotcakes, with their light brown crust, stood in the middle of the table. Later, Laila would learn that they were called *"piroshki,"* and they would become her second favorite Russian meal. For now, she called them *"potato thingies."*

Inna offered Laila a container of sour cream. *Thank goodness, not mayo.*

"It does really well with borscht," said Inna.

"No, thank you," declined Laila.

Inna scooped a dollop of sour cream and placed it on top of her soup.

Laila was halfway through her meal when she remembered something. It had been six months since Inna and Sergey arrived in Utah. Their behavior, manners, habits, and language had improved significantly. She decided to give it a try.

"Inna, do you want to tell me the '*Brother Bear*' story again? I'd really like to know what happened to that little bear."

Inna

I'M COOKING borscht and piroshki with potatoes today. It takes me several hours to get everything ready by the time Laila and Sergey come back from school. Sergey yells that he is not hungry but grabs a couple of piroshki and runs outside to play with his friends.

Yesterday, we drove to the Russian store that felt like stepping back in time. Familiar food names and brands, cheeses, sausages, spices, nuts, deli meats, and an overwhelming variety of sweets. Food that my American family would never appreciate or love as I do—sardines, herrings, dry fish, halva, and hard gingerbread cookies. We bought four bags of food. Also, we got some vegetables. I know that the cabbage and dill were grown and harvested here on American soil, but the fact that the produce was sold in the Russian store somehow made it fresher.

Laila goes to her bedroom and comes back to the kitchen table, where I serve her dinner. We bless the food, and I offer Laila a bit of sour cream for her borscht. She shakes her head.

It's a Russian thing—borscht with sour cream and piroshki instead of bread. Maybe one day she will try it.

My heart skips a bit when Laila takes her first spoonful to her mouth. I want her to like it. I want her to know that I'm trying really hard to adjust to this life. I want to share my culture and the food that represents it.

Laila swallows the soup, nods, and takes a bite of piroshki. I'm grateful she doesn't spit it into her napkin. She keeps eating, blowing on her spoon. I think she likes it. I sigh in relief and pick up my spoon.

My Russian borscht is salty, sweet, spicy, hot, tangy, and rich to the taste. It is not the same soup that my grandma would cook on her wood-burning stove. It has its own smell and taste. I enjoy every bite.

My American home smells like Russian borscht today. It is a different smell. It is a different taste. But it is good, and I think I will like it here.

HART AND SOUL

SEPTEMBER ROBERTS

Paranormal Romance

Ryan

*R*yan checked his watch. Again. The line backed up to the door, and no one seemed to care but him. What was it with these people? Why did they have to talk so much?

The Hart and Soul Café offered a variety of food, but it was their coffee that stood out. And only two people separated him from the thing he wanted most: the darkest, richest coffee in Salt Lake City. He wanted to push his way to the front so he could get on with his day, but he resisted the urge and waited like the model citizen that he was.

The man in front of him stepped forward.

"What can I get you?" the woman behind the counter asked, just like she asked everyone.

"I don't know, Morgan. What do I *need* today?"

The woman, Morgan, leaned forward, grasped the man's hands, and beamed at him. There was something radiant about the way she looked at him. She never looked at Ryan like that.

She closed her eyes for a moment and nodded. "You need a blueberry muffin and a cup of earl gray."

The man bobbed his head up and down like she had just suggested something life-altering.

"It's just tea and a muffin," Ryan mumbled. Maybe if he said it louder, he could break the spell between this poor sap and the woman.

Before the man left the counter, he took a big bite of muffin and sighed. "How do you always know?"

The woman's smile grew. "It's a gift," she said with a wink.

Honestly, who winks?

The man finally moved out of the way, and Ryan stepped up. He opened his mouth to order, but the woman spoke first, her radiant smile turning down a few notches.

"Coffee, black," she said in a deep voice that sounded like an approximation of his.

He snapped his mouth closed and nodded.

While she prepared his coffee, she said, "A little coconut oil would add so much flavor."

He opened his mouth to respond, but she went on.

"But you don't want that. Or cream. Or butter from grass-fed cows. Or, heaven forbid, sugar." She turned and placed his cup on the counter in front of him. "Just coffee. Black." She gave him a smile, but it was tight.

"Yes." He held out his credit card and waited for her to take it. Instead, she took his hand in hers. Even though he'd seen her interact with other customers like this, it was the first time she'd touched him.

Her glowing smile returned, the soft lines around her eyes deepening. "You need a lemon poppyseed muffin."

For some inexplicable reason, he didn't pull away. Instead, he smiled and leaned forward, drawn to her like a meteoroid drawn to Earth. Wait a minute. This is how she did it. She blinded her customers with that smile and got them to buy all sorts of fattening treats. Not today, Satan.

"No, thank you." When he removed his hand from hers, he left his credit card behind.

"Are you sure?" She narrowed her eyes as the smile dimmed again. "It'll make you happy."

Going to the gym made him happy. Getting to work early made him happy. Eating a muffin would not, in fact, make him happy. "No, thank you."

Morgan

As MORGAN SWEPT the café that evening, she couldn't shake the unsettling feeling she'd had since that morning. Since she'd spoken with Coffee, Black. Or, more accurately, since she'd looked into his face and noticed how handsome he was. Why was it that men aged so well? The gray at his temples made him look distinguished. The gray in her hair made her look like Broom Hilda.

He came every day at the same time and always only ordered coffee. She had loads of regulars, and they were all friendly. Except him.

There she was, dispensing happiness with every bite and Coffee, Black didn't want any of it. If people knew the truth behind her gift, they would be lining up around the block. The Hart women had to be careful when it came to how they used their magic and who knew about it. Her grandmother had made the mistake of letting the wrong people find out and spent most of her life trying to meet the extreme demands of the rich and eccentric. Turns out, some people aren't happy no matter what you give them. It was one of many cautionary tales told in her family.

When she had touched him that morning, she knew exactly

what he needed. The last time he'd had a lemon poppyseed muffin was when he was sitting in his grandmother's kitchen on a bright spring morning. Remembering it now made her smile as she emptied the dustpan. Sometimes the flashes of the past were so strong she got all wrapped up in them. That one had been warm and lovely, and she wanted to burrow deep into it. She wanted to show him that remembering those wonderful moments would make him happy as well.

Why couldn't she stop thinking about how attractive he looked when he smiled? It made her all warm and squishy inside. It was best he didn't experience joy around her. She didn't know what would happen if he smiled at her again. She probably wouldn't survive it.

She'd been practicing her gift her entire life. Her mother had shown her how to focus on the light. Never the dark. So, she honed her skills, dipped into the brightest, happiest memories, and helped people reconnect with them. She loved food, and she loved making people happy. Win-win.

Except Coffee, Black. She couldn't win with him.

Ryan

OVER THE NEXT FEW DAYS, Ryan watched Morgan closely. He thought about the smile on her face more than was probably healthy, as if the way she'd touched his hand had knocked something loose in his brain. On Friday, he waited for three entire minutes while a woman cried over her scone. He rolled his eyes and sighed.

"Thank you, Morgan," she finally said, wiping her eyes.

Morgan. The smiling, coffee-making, hand-holding woman.

The two women hugged, and a pang of jealousy hit him. The hug looked so intimate and warm.

Jealousy? Where had that come from? What did he have to be jealous of? He was fine.

The fact that he couldn't remember the last time someone had hugged him didn't mean anything. Wait. He knew. Five years ago, his mom had wrapped her arms around his waist and squeezed while the open casket holding his grandmother stood a few feet away.

"Ryan?"

They had gotten her makeup wrong. She never wore that much blush.

"Ryan?" His mom said his name softer, her voice closer now. No, not his mom. Morgan.

Pulled out of the worst memory of his life, he focused on Morgan, where she stood in front of him, her hand on his, a sad smile on her beautiful face. His sorrow threatened to swallow him whole, overwhelming everything else. Jealousy and impatience forgotten, Ryan let Morgan guide him away from the counter.

"Have a seat. I'll get your coffee for you." She led him to a table and let go of him.

He looked down at his hand and blinked. For some reason, he missed the warmth of her touch. It was the first time he'd sat in one of the café chairs, and he wondered why he hadn't done it before. The longer he sat there, the more he thought about his grandmother. This café smelled like her house. No wonder he'd been thinking about her so much.

"This will make you happy." She placed a bag on the table next to his usual cup of coffee. "On the house." She patted his hand gently and walked away.

Happy? How could he be happy when the memories of his grandmother's death held on to him so tightly? He inhaled deeply and closed his eyes. Inhale, hold, exhale, hold. Repeat. Just like his therapist showed him. It took a while before he felt like himself again. The ache in his chest was more manageable.

With his coffee and treat in one hand and his briefcase in the other, he walked to work. In all the years he'd been at the insurance agency, it was the first day he arrived late. The day was full of firsts.

He sat at his desk and stared at his computer screen, then at the bag Morgan had given him with his coffee. He expected to find a lemon poppyseed muffin, but to his surprise, he found a cranberry orange scone.

Would it be as good as the last ones he'd had with his grandmother? Should he eat it to find out? Morgan would ask him how it was the next time he got his morning coffee. If he didn't eat it, he'd have to explain himself. That would take forever. Better to eat it and prove that a scone wouldn't make him happy.

He'd never been so wrong in all his life.

Morgan

RYAN HAD BEEN on Morgan's mind all day. Again. That morning, despite her years of homing in on people's happiness, she couldn't avoid the grief spilling out of him. It had taken her a full minute to find a bright memory, something strong enough to balance him. And the two memories stayed with her all day. Light and dark. Joy and sorrow.

She flipped the last chair onto the table when the bell over the door chimed. Oops. She had forgotten to lock up again.

"We're closed," she called out as she turned. "Oh, it's you."

Ryan stood stiffly, his hand gripping his briefcase.

"Ryan? Are you okay?"

He tilted his head. "How do you know my name?"

"It's on your credit card, which I have seen every workday for the last year." She didn't mention why today had been the first day she'd used his real name. She felt connected to him now. He didn't need to know that she only called her friends by their names. Friends and customers were the same thing, right? "Can I get you something?"

"No. I'm sorry. I'll let you finish closing for the night." He turned to go, then stopped and added, "Thank you for earlier." His lip twitched in one corner. "You were right. That scone did make me happy."

"Oh?" She repressed a grin, but it was a hard thing.

"My grandmother was a fantastic baker. The day I graduated from college, she taught me how to make my favorite food in the whole world: cranberry orange scones." His mouth tipped up on both sides now. "We squeezed fresh oranges to make the glaze." He chuckled and closed his eyes, and when he looked at her again, they were full of happy tears. "We ate all of them and licked the pan afterward."

She had been right. She couldn't survive this man, smiling at her with his slightly crooked teeth and lips that looked so soft. "That sounds wonderful."

"It was." He sighed. "I miss her, and today, I got to be with her again. Thank you for that."

Moments like this made the loneliness of her life worthwhile. "Any time."

"For the record, your scones are just as good as hers."

Ryan

Monday morning, Ryan showed up a few minutes early to get his coffee. He'd spent the whole weekend thinking about his encounter with Morgan. The way she'd soothed him with her touch and reminded him of one of the happiest memories of his grandmother just when he needed it most.

He'd gone to live with his grandmother after high school, escaping his small South Carolina town and getting to know someone who loved him more than he thought possible. Those years had been the happiest of his life, which was probably why he still lived in Salt Lake City.

He needed to see if Morgan could do it again. It had absolutely nothing to do with the way she made his heart beat just a little faster or how adorable she looked with a bit of flour on her cheek. Not at all. This was all part of an experiment. If she could pick another food that made him happy, then he had to admit all these people were on to something. How could one person change his perspective so effortlessly with one bite? His usual impatience morphed into curiosity. Yep, just curiosity.

When it was his turn, he stepped up to the counter and basked in the warmth of her smile. It didn't matter if he believed she could magically pick the right food for each person. He couldn't help smiling back. Why had he spent the last year resisting her? His life was infinitely better when Morgan smiled at him.

"Nice to see you, Ryan."

"Hi, Morgan."

She narrowed her eyes. "How do you know *my* name?"

Heat flushed his cheeks. "I heard someone use it. I wasn't trying to eavesdrop. I just—"

"I'm messing with you. Everyone knows my name." Her shoulders shook with laughter. "Coffee, black. Right?"

"And?" he added quietly.

She raised her eyebrows as her smile grew. "And?"

"I was hoping you would tell me what I need," he whispered as he reached out to her, feeling ridiculous.

But she didn't hesitate to hold his hand in hers. If he was honest with himself, he would have to admit that getting to touch her was the highlight of this experiment. Within a few seconds, she said, "Today, you need a slice of spinach and cheese quiche."

Ryan typically skipped breakfast, but he barely made it to his desk before the urge to eat it overpowered him. The first bite took him back to a brunch he'd had with his parents at their favorite restaurant. His mom had let him have a sip of her mimosa, and he'd felt like a grown-up, even though he'd only been ten.

Morgan suggested something different every day for the next week. And each time, he smiled and laughed while he ate the food she'd made. There was something special about her. He didn't know how she did it, but it wasn't a fluke. No one could be right that often, and based on her dedicated clientele, she was right one hundred percent of the time. He'd seen enough to believe in her gift, as she called it. The experiment was over. Now he had to thank her with more than words.

He left work early again to stop by the café but found the door locked this time. Morgan swept her way around the tables, her hair falling across her forehead. He almost turned to leave when their eyes met, and a smile spread across her face.

She unlatched the door and invited him in. "Hi, Ryan."

"Hi, Morgan." His heart picked up, just like it did every time he interacted with her lately. "Do you need any help?"

"With what?"

"You tell me. I wanted to thank you for all the happy moments you've given me, and the only thing I can offer is my time, so put me to work. If you're comfortable with me being here, that is. With you. I mean, just us." What was it about her that made him blush and fall over his words?

"I'm very comfortable with you." Was she blushing too? That was too much to hope for.

Morgan

MORGAN BEAMED. She showed her love and appreciation by helping others, so the offer squeezed her heart. How had she ever thought she couldn't win with Ryan? "I still need to cash out, take care of the trash, and prep ingredients for tomorrow."

Ryan placed his briefcase on the table by the door. Then, he removed his suit jacket, folded it neatly, and rolled up his sleeves, showing off his strong forearms. "I'll finish sweeping, then take out the trash."

"Thank you."

"No," he said, taking the broom out of her hands. "*I'm* thanking *you.*"

She nodded and stepped into the kitchen, pressing a damp rag against her cheeks to cool them down. When she had things well in hand, she picked up a spare apron and brought it out to him. "You should protect your ..." She stopped and stared at him squatting over the dustpan. When had he loosened his tie and undone the top button of his shirt? "Clothes," she finished and averted her eyes as he stood. She should definitely *not* be watching the way his strong thighs flexed against his slacks.

"My hands are kind of full. Can you help?" He lifted his arms and turned around, presenting an even better view.

Morgan stepped up behind him and wrapped the apron with her café's name around his waist. Thank goodness it wasn't the kind that went around his neck. That would mean his face would be close. Close enough to kiss. She needed to stop all those thoughts. He was being nice. She was being inappropriate. Before she could think about how nice he smelled or how warm his back was through his clothes, she tied a bow in the strings and took four steps backward. "I'll be in the kitchen."

She'd been compiling a list of recipes to make the following day, so she set to work gathering supplies and ingredients. It made mornings more manageable.

"What are you making tomorrow?"

Morgan squeaked in surprise and put her hand over her heart. "I forgot you were here."

Ryan grimaced. "I didn't mean to scare you."

"It's okay. Not your fault. I was in my own head. That's how it always is when I'm planning the menu."

"How do you decide? Do your customers tell you what they want?"

"Something like that." It took a special kind of balancing act to anticipate what customers would need from day to day, even with her gift. "Blueberry lemon scones, bacon and cheese frittata, double chocolate muffins," she paused and thought back to the memory she'd glimpsed that morning when she'd touched his hand. "And cinnamon coffee cake."

"With a streusel topping?" His eyes went wide.

"Obviously." She grinned, and he reciprocated. When had he started to smile at her like that?

"I've never had your coffee cake before."

"I hope you'll like it."

"I like everything you make." A beautiful rosy flush spread across Ryan's cheeks. He cleared his throat and nodded at the garbage. "I already took care of the can under the register and by the door. Is this the last one?"

"Yes, thank you."

By the time she finished kitchen prep, Ryan had removed his apron and shrugged back into his jacket. "Thank you for letting me help. Can I come again tomorrow?"

"You don't have to."

"I want to." The smile on his lips was so sweet.

"Then yes, please come again tomorrow."

Ryan

THE CLOCK on Ryan's desk ticked down the hours until he could see Morgan again. Usually, he'd get so wrapped up in work that he didn't bother to leave until hunger forced him home. But now, he took shorter lunches and didn't take on extra cases so he could leave early to see her. He'd finished the last bite of his cinnamon coffee cake an hour ago, managing to savor it all day long as he went through house insurance claims. There was always at least one thing in her pastry case that he loved. Sometimes it felt like she baked just for him.

At five o'clock sharp, he stepped through the doors of the café. "It's me," he called out.

Morgan's voice came from the kitchen, "Be right out. Will you lock the door and come grab your apron?"

His apron. He liked the sound of that. He liked it even more when she put his apron on him, but he couldn't think of an excuse why he might need her help again, so he put it on himself.

They moved together just like they had the previous night, like they'd been doing it their whole lives. Like he could continue to do this for the rest of his life.

The realization slapped him upside the head, stopping him in his tracks. Until recently, he worked until seven or eight each night. But work didn't make him happy, not like this. Then again, how could denying homeowners coverage make anyone happy? Morgan had shown him how to find joy in simple things, and it changed the way he looked at his life.

"Are you okay?" Morgan frowned from her position behind the register.

"Yeah, just thinking about work." He liked feeling useful and being praised by his boss, but the actual work didn't fulfill him, and if he was honest, it never had. "How long have you been in business?"

"Fifteen years overall. Five at this location."

He whistled. "Does it make you happy?"

Morgan smiled and nodded. "I make people happy every day."

"Sure, but does it make *you* happy?" When she narrowed her

eyes, he went on. "I make my boss happy every day, but I think I hate my job."

"Oh, Ryan." The tenderness in her voice nearly broke him.

"I know, right? I just realized that. But what about you?" The thought of her going through the motions made him want to set the world on fire. When had those feelings started?

She sighed and seemed to really think about it. "I do. It's a lot of work, and my mornings are very early, but it's satisfying. When I see the look on someone's face after they've taken a bite of a muffin, it makes it all worth it."

"It makes *what* worth it?"

Morgan shrugged. "The loneliness. I never made time for more, and I'm just realizing that maybe I'm missing out."

"My grandmother warned me about that. She told me there were more important things in life than work. I never believed her." The addition of 'until now' didn't need to be said.

"She was a wise woman."

Ryan nodded. "She would've loved you. You're exactly—" He cut himself off just in time. He had been about to say that she was the kind of woman his grandmother wanted him to marry. Someone kind, funny, and warm. The kind of woman Ryan had stopped looking for years ago because she didn't exist. Except apparently, she did.

Morgan

"I'M EXACTLY WHAT?" Morgan said, wishing she could read his mind. She could practically see his brain short-circuiting.

"Like her. I was going to say you're just like her." That was definitely *not* what he was going to say, but she would let him off the hook this time.

Morgan laughed. "You only say that because my scones are as good as hers."

Ryan grinned, and the brightness of it knocked the air out of her lungs. "Don't let it go to your head."

"Too late. I'm going to be insufferable from now on." When their laughter quieted, she smiled at him. "Thanks for keeping me company. It's been really nice. And the help. I really appreciate all the work you're doing here."

"So, I can keep coming?"

Forever. She hoped he kept coming forever. "Yes, please."

TRUE TO HIS WORD, Ryan showed up promptly at five. Morgan looked forward to it more than any other part of her day—except maybe in the mornings when she got to touch him for a few seconds to find what he needed.

The temptation to ask him out became stronger each time they interacted, but the idea of him rejecting her was too much to handle. What if it made him uncomfortable? What if he stopped coming? Or worse, what if they went on a date and things went well? Eventually, he'd find out about her family, and it would be too much. She would scare him away, just like her last boyfriend. She had to tell him everything. If he stayed, maybe she'd get up the courage to ask him out.

With her heart in her throat, she watched the door from the coziest table in the café and waited.

At five, he stepped inside, locked the door, and was halfway through rolling up his sleeves when he finally looked at her. "What's wrong?"

"We need to talk." Seeing the panic on his face, she quickly added, "About my family." She gestured to the seat across from her.

Traces of panic remained, but curiosity overpowered everything else on his face. "I'm listening."

"I need you to keep what I'm about to tell you to yourself."

"I promise," he said without hesitation.

She swallowed hard and hoped she wasn't making a mistake. "My family is … special."

A wide smile turned up his mouth. "Of course it is. You're a part of it."

The compliment, paired with his smile, made her stomach flip. But she had to stay focused. To just get it out. She shook her head. "By special, I mean magic. We're witches." She had a family of personal shoppers, bartenders, and cooks. "We have the gift of happiness. Mine is linked to food."

"Magic food." He tilted his head.

"Not really. The food isn't magic. It's your connection to it that matters."

Ryan's eyes widened. "That's how you know. Every day for weeks now. You know exactly what to feed me."

"When I take a person's hand—" she reached out to him, and he placed his hand in hers without hesitation, "—I can sort through their memories. They shine like bright lights." She'd noticed his changing over the last few weeks. Instead of being singular memories, they were layered. Cranberry orange scones were tied to his grandmother and her now. She closed her eyes and focused. "I see snapshots of joy in your life. Sharing spaghetti with your cat when you were six. Dipping fries in a shake on a date in college." She laughed. "Your date thought you were weird."

He chuckled. "She did. My grandmother told me she wasn't worth my time. You can see all that?"

"I can." She hesitated to open her eyes, terrified of what she would find, but finally looked at him.

Ryan had wonder in his eyes. "You're magic."

"I am."

"You're a witch."

"A *good* witch," she emphasized.

"Witches exist."

Morgan nodded. "We do, and I trust you to keep that to yourself."

"I'll keep your secret." He rubbed his thumb against her palm. "Thank you for trusting me."

"Thank you for not freaking out." She laughed nervously. "That could've gone horribly. Believe me."

He frowned. "You've told someone before."

"Yes. And he didn't stick around for long after."

"That's why you're lonely."

"Yes." She hadn't opened up to anyone in years. It had always been safer to keep her secrets and accept that the joy in her life came through her customers. But Ryan changed everything.

"Why me? Why now?" His cheeks flushed.

"Because I like you, and I want to spend more time with you. And, before I ask the question I've been wanting to ask, I didn't want any secrets between us."

He leaned forward, closing the distance between them. "I don't have any secrets to share, so I think we're in the clear now. What's your question?"

Her mouth went dry, and it became nearly impossible to focus on anything other than his lips and the way his chest rose and fell just as quickly as hers. "Will you have dinner with me?"

"Obviously, yes." He smiled. "I have a question for you, too."

He said yes. To her. To a *date* with her. She wanted to sing and dance around the room, but that would have to wait. "What?"

"Can I kiss you?"

Stupefied, she nodded and leaned closer to him. When their lips met, a sigh escaped her throat. She'd been thinking about kissing this man for weeks now, and it was better than she dreamed it could be. Soft, sweet, and just demanding enough to let her know he wanted her just as much as she wanted him.

Ryan leaned back and let out a slow breath. "Are you sure you're not a magic kisser?"

Morgan laughed and squeezed his hand. "I don't think so, but we might have to try it again to check. First, dinner."

As if on cue, his stomach growled. "Where are we going?"

"To my favorite Indian place."

He stood and pulled her to her feet. "I've never had Indian food before."

Morgan grinned up at him. "I know. Tonight, you'll make a new memory. One that's just for us."

DOORS

J. ALAN GIFT

General Fiction

I was sitting propped up against pillows on one end of the sofa in the living room with my legs stretched out in front of me. My mom brought me a tray so I could eat without having to move my ankle. She also gave me another Percodan in response to my complaints about continuing pain. I was floating in a slightly hazy cloud.

The living room area was open to the kitchen, so sitting on the sofa was almost like being in the kitchen. I was flipping through a Life magazine with a picture of Sirhan Sirhan, Robert Kennedy's assassin, on the front cover. My brother Greg was sitting on a living room chair looking up words in the dictionary.

My mom, standing at the kitchen counter, finished filling four bowls with green salad and was filling four plates with pork chops, corn, and baked potatoes when my stepfather came in the door from the garage. He wiped his boots on the rug. He glanced at me and then looked at my mom.

"What did they say?"

"He may have fractured a bone in his ankle, or it might just be sprained. They wrapped it. He should be fine."

"What good is a lame boy?" he asked, laughing a little, continuing to look at my mom. "If he was a horse, I'd shoot him."

"Please don't talk that way, Jessie. It's not funny."

Greg went into the kitchen and sat down on the far side of the table. Behind him, the sliding glass doors revealed a gray, windy day. Thunderclouds moved toward us over the wheat fields beyond the backyard and stables. My mother put plates of food in front of Greg and Jessie. She stood a moment by Jessie as if listening for something.

"What do you hear?" I asked.

"Nothing."

She brought me a plate of food and some silverware. She sat down at the table opposite Jessie.

We never said a prayer before eating when Jessie was home, so we all started eating. Jessie started cutting his pork chop. "Banana Rocket was accepted for time trials at the Los Alamitos futurity."

"That's great," my mom said without enthusiasm.

"Well, don't get too excited about it. You might spill your drink or something."

"Have you been slipping today?"

"Why, am I slurring my words?"

I looked at Greg, and he looked at me for a moment.

"Thought maybe you had a drink or two with Banana Rocket's owner," my mom said. "She seemed especially pleased with your performance."

"I had a couple of beers. Nothing unusual." He looked around at us. "What're all the serious faces for? Just two beers, I'm fine."

"Ok, Jessie," my mom said as if putting the subject to rest.

"Can't a man have a couple of beers on a weekend? I haven't had a drink for six months at least."

"Some people can have a couple of beers," my mom said, "and some people can't."

"That's all I'm having!" Jessie said, looking at her. "That's it. I'm done, no more, nada más hoy, promesa!"

We continued to eat in silence. Jessie shook his head back and forth, apparently frustrated with our limited understanding. He took a few bites of food, then set his fork down on the table softly, looking like he was resisting an impulse to slam it down. He stood up, scooting his chair backward with another carefully controlled movement. He walked past me and down the hall toward the master bedroom.

We waited for the explosion. Loud complaining and slamming the bedroom door was his favorite, generally something like, "THIS!" slam! "IS!" slam! "GARBAGE!" slam!

After a minute or two of nothing happening, I figured he was going to keep it together for now, which could be a good thing or could be a bad thing. My mother, I'm sure, would have preferred the immediate acting out of his anger rather than a delayed explosion when it was just the two of them.

"Could I get another pain pill?" I asked my mom. "The last one's not doing anything."

"Already?"

"Maybe I need a bigger dose," I said.

Jessie, wearing newly pressed jeans and a black T-shirt that showed how ripped he was, came striding down the hall, through the living room, through the kitchen, and out the door leading to the garage.

"I'm going," he said, closing the door behind him.

He started his truck. The garage door opened. He backed out and drove away.

My mother stared out the sliding glass doors into the darkening sky. "He's under a lot of stress."

"Why do you always try to smooth it over?" I asked.

"It's been a while since the drinking," Greg said, talking with food in his mouth, something he usually did just because he knew it bugged me.

My mom picked up her plate and started clearing the table. "We should be thankful he hasn't been drinking,"

"Mom, why don't you sit down?" Greg said. "We're not done eating."

"I'm done, and Jessie is."

"These days, he's always taking off because he 'needs a little time,' even when he's not drinking," I said.

My mother carried plates to the sink. "If you showed him a little more respect, you would have a better relationship."

"Me respect *him* more!" I laughed. "Is that what he told you or something you figured out yourself?"

"Both." She started scraping uneaten food off a plate and into the disposal. "Greg, could you bring the other plates and glasses over when you're done?"

"He'd be glad to," I said.

My mom dropped something in the sink, then glared at me. "Can you ever give it a break, Scott?"

She turned back toward the sink and put both hands on the counter, then leaned forward as if bracing herself because she felt faint.

"What's wrong?" Greg asked.

"Nothing."

She took a deep breath, stood up straight, and walked out of the kitchen, down the hall, and into the master bedroom. She closed the door behind her. We didn't hear more until she reached the master bathroom. The volume of what happened next was a notch or two down from Jessie's explosions, but loud enough to hear without straining: "DIRTY!" Slam! "SLUT!" Slam! "SLUT!" Slam! Greg and I exchanged glances. We had never heard our mother slam a door or call anyone a slut.

"That was different," Greg said. Huge drops of rain from the darkening sky started pelting the sliding glass doors.

After a few minutes, Greg stood up and started clearing off what was left on the table.

"A paramour," he said.

"What's that?" I asked, "My vocabulary word for the week or something?"

"Look it up. Jessie has one."

"Just tell me what it means."

"You look it up. You always know everything."

"Just tell me!"

Greg set some dishes in the sink and turned to look at me.

"Jessie has a girlfriend!"

We were both silent.... The rain continued against the sliding glass doors. There was nothing but darkness beyond the rain. I heard, faintly, my mother crying in her bedroom.

Greg, with his jaw clenched and his face reddened, started gathering the remaining silverware off the table.

"Now what happens?" I asked.

He picked up a steak knife and looked at it for a few seconds, then he looked over at me, "We slit his throat."

When he was done clearing the table, he began rinsing the dishes. I was still sitting on the sofa with my tray, plate, glass, and utensils.

"Would you mind getting my dishes too?" I asked. "And would you bring me that bottle of pain pills the doctor gave me? Mom keeps forgetting."

FOUND IN TRANSIT

HOLLY CHILCOTT

Contemporary Non-fiction

"*W*e are in a *fucking* cathedral," I growl at a pudgy guy from my tour group through gritted teeth in something less than a whisper.

Confused, the sandy-haired young man stares hopelessly up at me, blinking eyes pleading for some explanation of what he'd done wrong. I glare at his disposable camera, with its ridiculously loud shutter and jackhammer of a winding mechanism. With a jerk of my head, my bulging eyes point at a sign printed in German, English, and French. *No Flash Photography.*

The pudgy guy quickly tucks his camera into his jacket pocket. He looks to me for what to do next, as though being a bitch to him meant that I'm the boss of these parts.

Shit. What am I doing? I think to myself. I haven't been here a full week, and I'm already burning bridges. For all his youthful and naive appearance, this guy could be an officer—commissioned or non-commissioned. Whether or not he's in my unit, I may cross paths with him sometime over the next four years while we're both stationed here. Even if he's just a cook or finance clerk, he could easily spit in my food or make sure my paychecks never hit my bank account.

This whole group is comprised of American service members stationed at the various barracks, bases, and outposts in the greater Frankfurt area. We have been instructed to behave ourselves with the utmost respect for local customs from the moment we boarded the tour bus this morning. I'm no authority figure, but the Army guides are doing a terrible job keeping these greenies in line.

I notice a few more GIs tagging along behind me. *Shit. Do they think I'm a guide, too? Just because I scolded someone?* Most of the group are fresh-faced teens, straight out of basic training. Even in their civilian clothes, they stick out like a sore thumb. I try to put myself in their place. Who wouldn't want someone to take them in hand and tell them what they should be doing? Still, I never thought being bitchy would make them imprint on me like a brood of ducklings.

That thought reminds me of my first week in Germany, three years ago. I had come to work as an Au Pair but wouldn't be meeting my host family right away. I had been completely on my own and totally immersed in the language and culture. Despite two semesters of college-level German language classes and the highest marks in class, the real-world accents and dialects had been as alien to me as Chinese. I'll never forget the humiliation of asking a shop clerk for a "breast" when I had meant to ask for a hairbrush. Maybe I should take it easy on these kids.

The pudgy one takes a place at my right elbow. I feel pretty bad for barking at him—he looks scared and humiliated.

"Sorry about that," I whisper over my shoulder as we continue through the cathedral.

He shrugs something like, "No worries."

We amble around aimlessly, admiring the beautiful wooden craftsmanship within the Mainzer Dom. It's a resplendent fall midmorning, and I've got this soft spot for medieval architecture. Each time I stop to read through a plaque, refreshing my German, a rail-thin Redneck kid sidles up and asks me what it says in his trailer park drawl.

"It's in English, too. Look ..." and I point out the various blocks of text in each of the Big Three, universal European tongues.

This annoys him, but he won't go back to the Army guides. *What does he want from me?* I may know the language, but this is my first time in Mainz, too. He peppers me with the odd personal question and regales me with bizarre stories about his cousins and hunting possums as we make our way through an ethereal garden in the cathedral's modest courtyard. The Pudgy Guy stays close, listening in on these unsolicited exchanges.

Before I know it, it's time for the tour to move on. We've already visited the Gutenberg Museum and this cultural focal point with its surrounding market square. That's about the extent of anything useful the tour could offer me.

"Now we're going to teach you how to use the buses and trains." Our guides begin herding us out of the cathedral, but I'm already a veteran of European mass transit.

"Hey guys, I'm gonna split off now. I already know all this shit. You should stick with the group," I try to shoo them off. All but Pudgy Guy and Redneck Ringo wander off to rejoin the tour. "Guys, I'm just gonna be wandering around, exploring."

"Didn't you say you was a nanny out here awhile back?" Seriously!? Who does Ringo think I am?

"Yeah, but ... don't you guys have to report back for formation or something?" I'm grasping for a gentle way to shake these newbs. No burning bridges!

"Not 'til tomorrah. We'd learn jus' as much from you as we would from that Army fella."

I shift on my feet and look around as if the answer to my little dilemma were walking by, and I could just flag it down. It's true—this is a free day for us to acquaint ourselves with the surrounding cities, culture, and transportation systems of our new host nation. The only reason to stay with the tour is to avoid getting lost.

Now the shy, reticent Pudgy Guy seems to grow in both boldness and amusement. "C'mon, girl ... it'll be an adventure. We'll buy you dinner." He smiles playfully, in a more refined Southern drawl laced with a familiar kind of ... lisp.

"Suit yourselves." I shrug, annoyed. What's so hard about saying 'no' to people? I've almost always traveled alone, ever since my first trip overseas, to Ireland, when I was nineteen. I'm not used to people wanting to share the journey, let alone make me their leader. "But it's not my fault if you get lost and marked AWOL tomorrow."

Pudgy Guy smiles with a pinch of triumph on his cheeks, and we walk toward the nearby bus terminal. There are maps of the region, with colorful lines indicating the various routes that connect Mainz with Wiesbaden and the surrounding suburbs to which our military bases belong. I scan the map for the word "Hauptbahnhof."

My only goal is to familiarize myself with the main train stations of the biggest cities in the area. The best shops, clubs, museums, and restaurants are almost always very close by. Living in Germany, as independent as I could be, had been my plan from the moment I switched from the Utah National Guard to active-duty Army three months ago. I already know the food in the chow hall is atrocious, and I want to learn my escape routes for when the monotony of Army life gets over-whelming. My unit is such a small battalion, and it's situated on a tiny base in the middle of wine vineyards in the remote village of Dexheim.

I tap the map to draw their attention to our destination. "We want to go to the main train station." Their clueless reaction forces my eyes to roll. "Say it with me, kids: HAUPT-BAHN-HOF."

They un-ironically repeat the complicated German compound word.

"Great! Now for the tickets. You can use the kiosk, or you can talk to the driver. Anyone wanna give it a shot?"

They both shake their heads at me. Pudgy is grinning from ear to ear.

"All right, then I'll translate." I guess it's better to play nanny than teach them to speak the language. I'm still chafed at being conscripted as their personal guide. I'd much rather be listening to my Depeche Mode CD on the Discman I just picked up at the Post Exchange last night.

When the bus arrives, I signal the guys to follow me. We file on behind a few locals. "Drei für den Hauptbahnhof bitte," I ask the driver for our tickets. I don't mind paying the couple of Euros, anticipating a free dinner at the end of this babysitting gig.

"First thing you've gotta know about Germany is: the hamburger may have come from here, but they don't care for them nearly as much as we Americans do. Oh, and don't go flaunting the fact you're an American. In fact, best to pretend you're Canadian." I'm beginning to settle into my new role as tour guide.

A robotic female voice rings out over the bus intercom after only a couple of stops. "Hauptbahnhof." The bus lurches to an abrupt halt. I look around, and the terminal is a glorious circuit of brick and cobblestone lanes in front of an elaborate stone plaza. The train station itself resembles what we American kids might mistake for the Met or some magnificent eighteenth-century courthouse back home.

As we cross the plaza heading to the train station, I spot a Turkish bistro situated on the bottom floor of a shabby brothel. I ignore the seedy commerce upstairs, as well as the strange looks I'm getting from the Turkish men on both sides of the counter, and I order three Döner Kebabs.

"These are basically the cultural equivalent of the hamburger to us, even though they're Turkish," I say as I hand the guys their kebabs. "They're the effing *best.*"

Ringo looks at me with the same blend of suspicion and confusion as the Turkish men. It isn't lost on me that those men know who's doing most of the "work" upstairs and that a woman is remarkably out of place in their dining room. My German host family had frequently complained to me about mass immigration and the resulting culture clash. Being accompanied by two men is likely the only reason I wasn't asked to order from the takeaway window outside.

I try not to notice as Ringo drops his kebab in the trash while I'm reviewing the transport basics with them and thoroughly enjoying my snack. Annoyed but stoic, I demonstrate buying tickets from the kiosk before explaining how to read them and find the right platform. "These are just regional trains, so there's no seating assignment. On longer routes, they'll have first, second, and third classes. Pay attention to where you're sitting, or they might boot you off the train."

I'm not sure how much of what I'm explaining to them is landing. I have to remind myself that none of this is my job. They're the ones who came to me. I don't owe them kebabs ... *they* owe *me*, I seethe. We settle in for a quick ten-minute trip between Mainz and Wiesbaden.

"Hey, you guys never told me your names," I point out as I lean into my seat. *Gotta build bridges, not burn them.*

"Private Grimes," Redneck Ringo says. "Tony."

"Hey, Tony. I'm Holly. Pleased to make your acquaintance." I smile.

Grimes looks at me with an expression that falls just short of hostility. *What the hell did I do to piss this guy off?! And if he doesn't like me, then why follow me around?* I shrug my eyebrows and turn to Pudgy.

"You can call me Joe." He smiles, and I notice he's suppressing his lisp now.

"Hey Joe ..." I sing the famous first line of the Jimi Hendrix song. We all look out the windows as the carriage rocks and sways along the tracks. The sun is dipping under its zenith, and I'm feeling unsure of myself. *What the hell am I doing with these guys?*

"So, you were a nanny out here?" Joe asks.

Oh, thank God, someone else is speaking. "Yeah, although they say, 'Au Pair.'"

"What's the difference?"

"No idea." I shrug with an awkward chuckle. "Maybe it means that I was a live-in nanny instead of a part-time employee."

"Oh! So, you lived with the family?"

"Yeah, they had a little room in their basement for me. Honestly, I did more house chores than I did work with the kids."

"So, them folks just wanted an American servant, eh?" Grimes scowls.

The kid has a point. "That's what it felt like. Almost like it was some kind of status symbol."

"They was just lookin' for payback, I s'pose," Grimes sighs.

"Guess so." I shrug and look back to Joe.

"Still, that's really cool. You got to live in a foreign country and soak up the culture."

"Yeah, I mean, the mother of the family I worked for was a chef. Even if she was an overbearing bitch, I did learn to cook some pretty incredible food. And they took me around to markets and festivals. We even went shopping for fresh vanilla beans in Switzerland."

I hear Grimes sigh hard and ignore him. At this point, only

Joe has the right to resent me, yet he's the one being pleasant and engaging.

"So, Joe, what's your MOS?" If we can't talk about culture around Grimes, I suppose I can fill the awkward silence with Army chit-chat. One's Military Occupational Specialty is as good a place to start as any.

"Dental Hygienist." Joe smiles with full awareness of the oddity of his profession in a war-fighting context.

"Wow, that's gotta be pretty chill," I exclaim. "Never really thought about it, but we need dentists as much as we do medics," I giggle.

"Yep! I was a dental assistant in the civilian world. I figured I could still serve my country, even if I don't end up deploying."

"Well, fingers crossed I never have to deploy, either. I'm a supply tech. Nice, cushy desk job. I hope." A kind of nervous vibe washes over Joe and me. The whispers of war have been growing louder in the year since 9/11.

Grimes almost snorts as he heaves another derisive sigh. "Truck driver. Someone's gotta get the supplies to the front." I squirm under his implication of my cowardice.

The train gives a jolt as we make our final approach to the Wiesbaden main station. Not wanting to assume anything, I point out to the guys how the other passengers are gathering around the doors that will open onto the platform. For all I know, neither of these Southern boys has ever been on a passenger train.

"I wanna stop by a snack shop and see if they have any of those enormous chocolate bars I used to get in Switzerland," I tell the guys as I lead them out of the station. There's a string of taxis outside, but I assure them it's better to explore on foot. "You get a much better grasp of the lay of the land this way."

Grimes broods visibly as he follows us around a little grocery market while Joe and I talk. *With which one of us does he have the bigger problem?* I share fun little tidbits about the best snacks and the notorious Aldi checkout girls—who will throw your food on the floor if you don't bag it fast enough. I lead the guys around from shop to shop, through little parks, and past some old Roman architecture, not quite knowing, myself, exactly what we're looking at.

I do my best to translate plaques on statues and glean bits and pieces of the history of the area. "Wiesbaden," in German, translates to something like a countryside hot spring. This place was used, during the Roman occupation, as a kind of spa resort.

By dinnertime, we identify some interesting prospects for future exploration, but we're all ravenous. If ever there were a situation in which I'm the one needing guidance, it's the question of where to eat. I spot a taxi stand and pick a random driver to strike up a conversation with.

"Do you know any good places to get dinner around here?" I ask the driver in my less-than-fluent German.

"Yes, there is a great Tandoori restaurant I can take you to. Very close," the driver responds in equally novice German and a familiar accent. It's so surreal, getting restaurant recommendations from another non-native.

With no idea what Tandoori is, I'm up for an adventure. "Great! Take us there!" I'd rather pay for a short taxi ride than struggle through the language barrier to get directions. For the first time, Grimes's expression is more wonder than grave disapproval. Perhaps he heard what I heard in the driver's accent.

When we arrive at the restaurant, Joe insists on paying the driver. I thank the man and wish him a lovely evening. A jolly Maitre d' in a neatly wrapped turban greets us and ushers us to a table. Now, it makes sense why the driver recommended this place - Tandoori is a sort of Indian barbeque.

I feel out of place in such an elegant-looking establishment. There are crystal glasses, highly polished flatware, and *cloth napkins.* I've eaten at a lot of nice places back in the States, but never have I ever used *cloth napkins.*

We order a bottle of red wine and munch on complimentary pita chips, fresh naan, and bread sticks. I'm surprised when, as I'm struggling to read or order in German, the waiter effortlessly switches over to English and helps me pick an interesting curry dish I have never tried before. Joe follows my adventurous lead, but Grimes sticks with a simple plate of grilled meat and veggies.

We exhaust our supply of appetizers over a brutally protracted wait for our entrees, and I remember something else from my time as a nanny. In Europe, eating out isn't a perfunctory activity, it is a whole experience unto itself. That meant that, for the most part, the wait staff left you undisturbed to enjoy the food and conversation with your companions. Sadly, our muted small talk is painful and awkward at first. Grimes's attitude, so far, had made any truly interesting subjects almost taboo. That is, until the wine set in.

"Why d'you talk differnt when you's talking to Holly than when you's talking to other folk?" Grimes asks Joe, approaching the right blood alcohol content to finally express what, it seems, has been plaguing his mind most of the day.

I'm in no better a state when I blurt out, "He's probably worried they'll think he's gay!"

Desperation in the look Joe shoots me brings memories screaming into my mind. Memories from my junior year in high school. A real fear of being lynched had become a permanent fixture in my chest as I stalked the hallways, wondering what the popular kids knew about me that I didn't.

Back then, I had never thought of myself as much more than a tomboy. To the "cool kids," however, I was "butch" and "queer" —descriptors I had barely heard before, let alone applied to myself. It was a subject I had simply given little to no thought about. The bullies had largely ignored me when I spoke up about all the Mexican jokes they made right in front of me. So, why was *this* worth their notice? Their attention to me had been, in my mind, curiously selective.

Joe practically blinks in morse code at me, and even in my tipsy state, the message is clear. *Don't ask, don't fucking tell!!!* I should know better. Grimes simply isn't the one to be this casual with.

"Damn! I'm thirsty!!" I blurt these a bit louder than my last words, trying to snatch those back out of the air as if they hadn't yet floated into Grimes's inebriated ears. "What the heck is *rose water?*" I snatch the wine list off the table and flourish it around idiotically.

The waiter overhears my outburst and struts over to explain. He seems truly baffled when I ask whether they have ice water. We're all fascinated to learn that Europeans—most people, actually—don't drink plain tap water. Ice is even more foreign a concept to the waiter. So, I order a glass of the rose water, along with a round of plum wine for the whole table.

The rose water is a bitter, diluted sort of essence of the flower. It tastes about the same as it smells and comes in a small crystal tumbler. Washing it down with the plum wine is really not the way to deal with the aftertaste. It is, however, very useful in helping redirect Grimes's focus.

I splutter and make a bit of a scene about the potency of the plum liquor, secretly trying to drown all memory of the verbal catastrophe I had clumsily dodged. It's not long before we're all giggling, and Grimes proclaims us his new best friends in Germany.

Joe and I put Grimes in a cab after dinner and send him on his merry way back to the Wiesbaden barracks. Joe isn't assigned to the same unit as Grimes, but he will need to report to the same base later. I, on the other hand, have a long train ride back to Dexheim. If I'm lucky, there will be a taxi I can take from the village to my base. More likely, however, I'll have plenty of time to walk off the wine and listen to music on the footpath that winds its way right up to the front gate.

Joe offers me his arm, and we stroll lazily back to the Wiesbaden Hauptbahnhof. In our circuitous exploration of the area, we had been fortunate enough to end up at a restaurant that was situated on a street that connected almost directly to the train station. The Maitre d' assured us it's a left turn five blocks down.

"I'm really sorry. I didn't mean to out you like that," I fall all over myself, apologizing now that it's safe to do so.

"Don't worry about it. That was a nice save, by the way." He smiles at me with real warmth.

The conversation deepens as we huddle together under the starry late-September sky. It turns out Joe is not only the mild-mannered Army dental hygienist from Mississippi, with whom I've come to acquaint myself throughout the day. He is also a talented singer and performer. He admires strong women and is more than happy to emulate and pay homage to them with his stage persona: Sabrina Starr.

"When we get out, I'm coming to one of your shows!"

Joe walks me all the way to the platform and kisses my cheek before I get on the train. This is my first time experiencing a true Southern gentleman, and I blush, knowing I'm safe with this man. In the years since high school, I have been desperately trying to please people, to be what I'm *expected* to be. Joe had accepted me for who I am. *It's going to be an adventure figuring out who that really is,* I think.

I remember my Depeche Mode CD and slide my headphones over my ears. I skip through the tracks and settle on "Somebody." The rhythmic clacking and swaying of the carriage along the rails compounds with the remnant buzz from the wine, and I settle into a dreamy stupor that lasts even after I exit the train at the Dexheim station.

The whole journey back to my barracks, I smile to myself at

how much fun I'm going to have now that I've found a true friend. We've exchanged phone numbers and have plans to spend our free time exploring together. I may be in Europe on a military tour, but it isn't going to be a grind. At least on weekends, I'll be able to share my adventures with a kindred spirit.

A TASTE OF LIFE

NANCY GRANDUCCI

Memoir

I grew up in the '40s and '50s, in a small southern New Jersey town. When my dad wasn't home for dinner (shift work), my mom let my brother and me watch Sky King Ranch Pilot and the Lone Ranger. And no, it wasn't on TV, but we did look at the radio box. Really. Look at old pictures of families gathered in a living room. Everyone is facing the radio, usually encased in a wooden cabinet. Mom was proud of that piece of furniture. The day Dad took the back off to repair it and found a small car radio, he was not impressed.

When Dad was home for dinner, we ate together at the kitchen table. Every night. Dad pulled into our driveway (with our only car) at four-eighteen, and dinner was on the table at five o'clock. My brother and I took our places promptly, with hands washed and hair combed. Dinner included some variation of beef, pork, ham, or chicken, always potatoes, usually a vegetable, either fresh from the garden, frozen, or canned at home, bread, and butter, also. Mom fixed rice once. My dad tasted it, then asked for potatoes.

We had a large 'victory garden,' as it was termed in the '40s. We raised tomatoes, green and pole beans, corn, asparagus, strawberries, potatoes, and some herbs. From a grape arbor, Mom made jelly, and our apple trees produced delicious pies. Plus, there was a swing hanging on stout rope with a wooden seat. I spent thousands of hours swinging, usually singing a babble of songs I made up.

Even as young as four, my brother and I were taught to 'string' green beans, open lima bean pods, and pick ripe tomatoes from our half-acre garden. Summer mornings were often spent under the trees in the backyard, snapping a bushel or two of green beans for Mom to freeze. An afternoon reward was a trip across the street to the gas station for a soda or popsicle. I was the oldest of the five kids in the neighborhood, so I went to the store and had to remember what flavor each wanted.

I learned to tell the summer weeks by what was on the table. When the green beans, which I disliked, were 'in season,' that's what we ate. By August, there was more variety when we could pick lima beans, tomatoes, and corn. A family favorite was succotash, a combination of lima beans, corn, butter, and heavy cream. Milk, with cream on the top, came in glass bottles left every morning in the metal box by the back door. In the winter, the cream would freeze and pop the cardboard top off the bottles. My taste buds come to high alert at the memory of spooning out that frozen cream. Not too much, for the cream was for Dad's coffee.

Meat came from a butcher shop. I liked to go there because he would let me come into the back, where there was sawdust on the floor, and let me watch as he put our mixture of meats into the grinder.

In the small town just north of ours, Tuesdays were Cow Town Days. It was similar to a giant farmer's market. Wandering through the aisles in the big, covered barns, you could buy anything from school clothes to watermelons. There were pigs, steer, and fowl for sale in the area outside if you wanted to raise or butcher your own. Young ones were often bought by 4-H'ers. When we went, Mom liked to get meat, especially bacon, from the Amish stall. The smiling women in gray dresses and little white caps fascinated me.

In the evenings, there was a Cow Town Rodeo. A strange thing for southern New Jersey! Story was that the owner of the land had gone on a trip to Texas and was so fascinated by rodeos, he wanted to bring that experience to his hometown. My uncle went to Texas to see what it was all about. He came home with pointy-toed boots and promptly bought land and some horses to ride. Mom said the rodeo was too dusty and not a place for a lady. So I only went once or twice, but my brother got to go often with my dad and uncle.

At eleven, I was so proud when I was given the butcher knife to cut asparagus for dinner. It meant my dad trusted me to judge when a stalk was ripe, and Mom trusted me not to cut off my toes. My dad had exacting methods for all these garden chores. Did we grumble? Sure, we were kids, so playing was more important. Did we complain? Ah, nope, no way, are you crazy? Although my mom often said, "You just wait till your father comes home," in retrospect, I realize my father never laid a hand on us except for hugs. We were raised to mind our elders. There was no social media where we could gain support for talking back. It wasn't until high school that I had friends I could complain and commiserate with.

A chore I disliked was going into the cellar to get a pan of potatoes for dinner. A scary place, that cellar. Dark, with only one light bulb hanging from the ceiling. Toward the end of spring, before the new potatoes were available, some of the things in that tall, dark basket were soft, rotten, and smelly. I hated sticking my fingers in one. If I had gone slowly, I could have avoided the bad ones, but I was always in a tearing hurry to get out of the cellar. My brother teasing me for being a 'scaredy-cat' didn't help. Eventually, I convinced my parents I was more helpful to Mom in the kitchen, so brother dear got to wrestle with the potatoes. To my dismay, he never complained. But years later, I learned that he didn't much like the cellar either.

At a young age, I learned to set the table and make sure bread and butter were next to my father. I graduated to helping my mother stir stuff—making iced tea in the summer or pouring milk for my brother and me.

One of my first questionable food experiences was in the elementary school lunchroom. The smell of a pb&j sandwich wafted out as I opened my lunch box. I discovered that when one of the mean boys on the school bus knocked my lunch box on the floor, the glass bottle in my new thermos broke and ruined my milk. But my chicken and lettuce sandwich wrapped in waxed paper and my cookies were okay because the thermos hadn't leaked.

The kids with 'home lunches' sat in the back of the lunchroom. The teachers sat with their classes in the front. I preferred to take my lunch because it tasted better, but also because we had less supervision at those back tables. We traded. My orange for a cookie. Half a ham sandwich for a chicken leg.

In the line for 'bought' lunches, we were handed a plate and a small carton of milk. A hot dog in a roll, smothered in ketchup, smooshed onto the side of a plate of runny creamed corn? My five-year-old solution was to pick up just the hot dog to avoid the soggy roll—with my fingers. Big no-no. I dislike ketchup to this day.

Then there was the high school cafeteria. "Thirty-five cents, please." Frustrated with the need to ask my parents for money all the time, I made a budget. My father was impressed as I explained it would be better for me to manage things without his need to dole money out to me. I became the proud owner of an allowance of five dollars a week. What was on my list? Well, I needed fifty cents for my piano lesson, thirty-five cents a day for school lunch, fifty cents for church tithe, a movie (fifty cents plus ten cents for a box of Good and Plenty). Sixty cents for a tuna sandwich, pack of Nabs, and a vanilla coke for Friday lunch with my girlfriends. Not much left.

One of my friends scoffed at my allowance. Said she could get more by just asking. But my mom had a strict budget, and by Thursday or Friday, if I asked for money for, say, a movie, the answer would be no.

But I did have a plan, which I suspect my mom knew of. Of course, that meant my dad did also. But I thought I was so smart! My grandmother, who ran a small boarding house, lived two blocks from the high school. She always had lots of food and invited me to come for lunch any time. So, except for pouring rain or bitter cold, I freeloaded at my grandmother's table, saving those precious coins for maybe a record, sixty-nine cents for a 45—Johnny Mathis, Nat King Cole, Elvis all tops, or the weekly sock hop for thirty cents, or maybe a lipstick, of which my dad did not approve.

One of my favorites from my grandmother's lunches was a do-it-yourself mixture. The base was mashed potatoes layered with bits of pork, maybe leftover vegetables, sauerkraut for the boarders, and chopped hard-boiled eggs. My uncle liked to pour vinegar on it. He always offered the cruet of vinegar to me with a wink and a grin because he knew I would say, "No, thank you." A game we played.

By now, I had realized many foods were not as good as those from my dad's garden.

My brother and I were held to high academic standards. Our parents were determined their children would 'do better' when they grew up. Have choices they didn't have. Dinner was time for Dad to 'talk' to my brother and me. Well, I can brag that I set the bar high while my brother was determined to skip over, under, or through it. The half-hour lecture when I had an A-instead of an A on a report card still replays in my ears.

My dad's vision for me was to become a secretary. Well, my typing was atrocious, and that was on a good day. I was easily bored, disliked sitting at a desk, and was stifled by routine. There you have it. Life in a secretarial pool sounded like a straitjacket.

I wanted to attend college so bad I could taste it. I knew my grades gave me choices, but I would have to score a scholarship to make it happen. My dad was adamant that there was only money for one of us to go to college, and it was for my brother because "he would have to support a family, blah, blah."

My school counselor helped with applications. I was accepted at four colleges, but only one offered a scholarship. A fairly prestigious women's college in Pennsylvania, where interestingly, my high school principal and biology teacher had attended. Was I herded in that direction? Perhaps. If so, I am ever grateful to them.

On the first day of class at college, a woman raised her hand and responded to a question, then others chimed in. The comments were respected and encouraged by the professor. I caught others' eyes as we glanced around in glee. In the late '50s, the opportunity to study in classes where a woman's voice was heard was not the norm. Now, we were no longer being ignored, patronized, or placed below our male peers. Some asked, don't you miss men at the school? Ah, nope. Men are everywhere, and I just didn't need them in my classes for the next four years. Not having to avoid a guy in the library stacks? Precious.

Now, don't get me wrong. Men were great for dinner and a dance, but I had no desire for a permanent attachment ... well, maybe someday. But first, I had places to go and things to do.

And I did have fun. Times Square on New Year's. A senior English seminar with Robert Frost. Rooting for horses at the

Preakness Race in Baltimore, one of the three races for the Triple Crown Sweepstakes. Shaking hands with young Senator John Kennedy. Watching the Army-Navy football game at Penn and dancing at the Delt House.

Our college dining room was lovely, overlooking a babbling brook. The food was sufficient to satisfy hunger, although certainly not gourmet. Monday was what we termed 'mystery meat,' slices of something brown or gray covered in gravy. The coffee, which came from huge drip urns, was great on Sundays. By Saturday, it was a bit sludgy. Legend said it was drained through the gardeners' socks—you get the picture. Veggies were a far cry from my mom's frozen green beans. I had no idea spinach came in cans! One dessert, called Perspective because it was served on weekends when girls came to visit the school, was delicious. A combo of layered chocolate, pudding, and whipped cream.

After college, I worked for five years as a credentialed teacher. Two years in Baltimore and three when, tired of scraping ice off the car windshield, I moved to Orlando. When I discovered Florida was creating an Educational TV station, I was excited. Distant learning was a future I wanted to be part of. I didn't have the experience to be a TV teacher when the call went out to apply for jobs there, but I was hired as a teacher's assistant. Providing a professional TV class five days a week was an exhausting schedule for the teachers. In a classroom, time for a lesson was flexible. Not so with a TV. Each lesson had to fit the time period and be as professional as possible. It was my job to locate materials a teacher needed, plus provide everything from copyright credits for textbooks to acknowledgments for local stores that donated materials. My day might require finding a quote for the English teacher, locating a live rabbit for the science man, or even escorting visitors around the station. Every day was hectic and always a challenge, but I loved it. There was excitement in the air in this brand-new TV station.

But all work and no play ... a colleague dragged me to a cocktail party. I heard a wonderful laugh and spotted a glorious man on the far side of the room with a sigh. He was way above my reach. He joined my group sometime later, where we were avidly discussing "What's your sign?" Turned out Mr. Handsome was a Cancer. When he said his birthday was the 6th, and I said mine was also, he scoffed, "Who told you to say that?"

"My mother," I shot back. Annoyed by his rudeness, I turned away to join another group. That guy clearly needed someone to take him down a few notches. I looked for my friend to tell her I was leaving. A few minutes later, Mr. Jerk was at my side.

"Please, I'm sorry. Can I apologize by taking you to dinner to celebrate our birthdays?"

This man, Joe, was a pleasant dinner companion. He treated me with Kahlua for my coffee. I'd come a long way from pb&j.

Next time I saw him at a party, he came right to me, stayed by my side, and asked me for another date. Weeks and several dates later, we stopped at a drive-in for coffee after a movie. I dropped something on the floor of the car. When I leaned up, his face was right there, coming closer. The kiss was soft, almost like a question. It was enough to rock my senses, but his whisper, "I've wanted to do that for weeks." *Well, Nellie, close the gate. What are we going to do with this complication?* By now I was twenty-three and had kissed enough frogs to realize this guy was a prince. But I still had no interest in anything serious.

Many more dates and months later, I went home to New Jersey for a summer visit. Since our families lived about three hours apart, I invited him to meet my family. By now, most of my high school friends were married, but I had never even brought a guy home, so my mom was in a dither. My dad invited my aunt and uncle, and of course my brother, who had finally found a college he didn't want to flunk out of, was there. I should have realized this was to be an inquisition.

Mind you, my family was devout protestant stock. So, I

brought home: an Air Force pilot, seven years older, divorced, raising a three-year-old daughter, Catholic, Italian, and a Republican. Any one of them would have been enough, but as all that came out at dinner, my dad was, for once, speechless.

Let me set the scene for this. The men in my family took it as a challenge to see who ate the most. My man was a quick study. I had never seen him eat so much, but his praise of my mother's fried chicken won her heart. His 'sins' didn't matter; mom liked him, and the menfolk better mind their manners.

So, I felt it necessary to prove I was a good cook. Mind you, I could bake anything. Blue ribbons from the state fair for cakes and cookies, all compliments of 4-H. I'd sat on our kitchen stool for hours, talking to my mom while she cooked dinner. But other than stirring something on the stove? Nope.

So, back in Orlando, I invited my guy over for a home-cooked dinner. His mother was also a virtuoso in the kitchen, so I wanted to prove … something, I guess.

I'd never cooked a complete dinner before, so I poured over my two cookbooks and decided to challenge my mom's chicken. When Joe arrived, the kitchen smelled wonderful. But nothing was getting done at the right time—yeah, timing is everything— so I was in a hurry to get things on the table.

This next is not for the faint of heart. I reached into the oven to proudly extract the lovely baked chicken. Without thinking, without hot pads. The first trickle of pain told me immediately this was a dumb idea but was trumped by my desire to 'not drop the lovely chicken.' I kept hold of that pan long enough to get it to the counter. Wailing by then. The next minutes were hands in cold water and ice, jumping up and down with tears of pain and embarrassment.

"Sweetie, you didn't have to do this." Arms around me, a whisper in my ear. "Let me take you away from all this."

Stunned in my fog of pain, I wasn't sure what he meant. A proposal? Take me away … from what? My pain. Yeah, great idea. From the kitchen, no, no, he hasn't even tasted my chicken. From this life? Ah, no, no, NO. I love my job at the TV station. I've applied to be one of the teachers next year. The job is great, but the pay will not support me. I still have miles to go.

My takeaway? I had just demonstrated my poor cooking abilities, so why a proposal? Plus, I knew he could easily find a domestic goddess. So, why me?

My mom had left nursing school to marry my dad. She had no skills for the marketplace. If she lost my father, she would have no way to support a family. I was determined not to be trapped in a world that only valued women as teachers, nurses, wives, or if they could pass a typing test. I wanted a career where I could support myself. I never wanted to depend on a man. Plus, I wanted to see something of life before I 'tied' myself down.

So, my answer was a fumbling "I like you a lot. It's not you. It's me. I just don't want to get married."

I say I fumbled because I really liked this man, though I suspected it was bordering on 'in love.' I regretted that turning down his offer would send him off to find someone else, someone who could cook.

"That's okay. I'm not going anywhere," he said as he got more ice out of the freezer. *This man does not kiss or act like a frog. What do I do with a prince?*

He suggested a couple more times over the next year that we would be good together, but he never pressed me. We went to parties, dinner and dancing, cookouts at a secluded beach, often with Laura, his young daughter. I loved him and his daughter but still didn't want marriage.

Still. *Wanted to do this for three weeks ...* and *Let me take you away ...* lingered in my mind and found a way into my heart. I wondered if this military pilot and a wannabe TV teacher could ever mesh.

The slight news mutterings about some place on the other

side of the world didn't register. Until my guy, by now an Air Force Captain, got an assignment to Viet Nam. Yes, it was a place; I looked it up in an atlas. And folks were shooting, like in a war, there.

One more time, "Please, marry me before I leave."

"When is that?"

"Six weeks from now. In twelve days, I need to report to a different base."

My first reaction was to wait until his year in Nam was over and marry when he returned. With some prying, I learned that he could extend his tour for years on a dangerous mission several pilots had already died performing. I asked myself the hard questions. What if I never saw him again? What if he never came back?

So I said 'Yes' in hopes that marriage would somehow tether us together. In nine days, we arranged a wedding—church, gown, flowers, music, reception. It all happened like magic. His mom fixed chicken cacciatore for a small rehearsal dinner with my parents and our two attendants. Joe winked at me and announced he had the three best chicken cooks in the world at his table. My dad looked at me, stunned, but my mom just beamed a smile.

We honeymooned at an air base on the gulf. I fixed chicken several times in that small apartment during the five precious weeks we had there, remembering the hot pads. And I learned a secret. My new husband knew his way around a kitchen as well. Then he was gone.

I moved into his home with his mother and our daughter Laura, who was a delightful five-year-old basket of ornery. My mother-in-law, in addition to keeping me sane, taught me how to time everything for dinner, how to cut up a whole chicken, and how to tell round steak from prime rib. I realized the year would be a constant worry. I had resigned from my job at the TV station and found a teaching position at a nearby high school, which kept the jitters at bay during the day.

My Christmas present was tickets to Hong Kong for a second honeymoon. From Orlando, I flew to San Francisco overnight. The next morning it was the champagne flight to Hawaii. On the long flight to Hong Kong, we had a chicken dinner at every stop for refueling. That was 'back in the day' when flying was a treat you dressed up for, and the food was great.

We celebrated with dinner at the top of the Hong Kong Hilton, with more lovely Kahlua, which had become a ritual for us.

One night we were out for a walk and happened upon a Chinese restaurant. The menu was in Chinese, which the waiter couldn't explain in English. By pointing to something a waiter served to a nearby table, we managed to order a large bowl of rice with shrimp on top and a sheep eye in the middle. After my husband explained it would be an insult not to eat it, he gulped it down with nary a pause. My hero.

There was live entertainment by a Philippine band, with sly jokes from a comedian ... about America ... in English. Interesting that no one would help us read the menu, but everyone laughed at those jokes. At the first jab about something our President had done, there was tension in the audience. But when we laughed, the jokes were on. I'll always remember that foreign restaurant. Something about laughter brings people together.

Next, we flew to Saigon for a week. So many different foods. I loved onion soup and ordered it whenever it was on the menu. The best I ever had was at a restaurant in Saigon, Caruso's. It came out of the brick hearth so hot the steam reddened my face when I broke the crust on the top. One of my memories from the villa there was the young Vietnamese woman who followed 'madam' about with a tinkling glass of iced tea.

On the flight to Bangkok, the plane strayed over Laotian territory, and they demanded we land. I was told to pull my scarf down to hide my eyes and hang on to my passport. Soldiers boarded the plane armed with Uzis. That was one of the most terrifying moments of my life. I had visions of life in rice paddies. But after stomping around and yelling at the pilot, they left, and we continued to Bangkok.

More exotic food. One dinner was set in a jewelry store, where my husband purchased a beautiful star sapphire necklace for me afterward.

The flight back home was marked with tears. A few things his friends let slip brought home to me how dangerous the job of Forward Air Controller was. He flew a small plane low to draw enemy fire, then radioed the position so the ground troops could find them. It was a long four months until his tour was over.

Back home, my mother-in-law and I babysat my two-year-old niece for a few weeks. We laughed as the sweet child firmly announced "bugs" as she chucked the raisins from her bran cereal on the floor. That helped a bit with the worry, as did my job teaching history to highschoolers.

I took Laura to New Jersey to visit her grandparents. My mom enjoyed making cookies for her first grandchild. My dad taught her to pick tomatoes. He also let her 'help' scale fish he had caught in the Delaware River. That required a bath! Laura was very proud of 'my fish' for dinner that night, accompanied by 'my tomatoes.'

Then Joe was home, and we began a kaleidoscope of years as our family grew with five children, an assortment of cats and dogs, and always memories of food. We spent some summers at his family's cottage on the Severn River in Maryland. My earliest memory there is the scent of Old Bay seasoning as crabs were steamed in the huge pot, newspapers thick on the table, and crabs dumped in the middle. I was shown how to 'pick' them with a mallet, wooden block, and a nutcracker. There was also melted butter, a large bowl of rolls, and iced tea or cold beer. Only one rule. If you touched it, it was yours. No hefting one to see how heavy it was. Because of the way crabs change shells, the largest was not necessarily the one with the most meat inside. I cherish the memories of crab for lunch.

Early mornings we fished for 'sunnies' for breakfast and went crabbing for lunch. We sent kids off to classes for summer things: swimming, tennis, golf, mostly messing around being children in a safe environment in the 70s. I halted my search for the best onion soup; the crab cakes at the Chesapeake House on the bay in Annapolis were not to be missed.

Having a military husband meant we moved about. I learned to deal with hurricanes in Florida, tornadoes in Illinois, and earthquakes in Utah, with all the different local foods and recipes.

One April 14th in Illinois, my husband and I were upstairs in the dining room of the Officer's Club for a formal dinner. A tornado alert had sent families in the base housing area to the designated shelter, which was the basement of the club. So, pouring rain, wet people and dogs, and temperatures in the high 80s. But the air conditioners could not be turned on until the 15th. Don't ask me why the dependents were down in the 'secure' area, but our headquarters dinner continued despite thunder and flickering lights. I don't remember the food served that night, but I do recall the sweat dripping down my back.

When my husband retired in 1975, we settled in Utah, where I learned to cook salmon and venison. A friend, who termed himself the Old Sheepherder, shared his sourdough and taught me to cook pancakes and sourdough biscuits over a grill. We had a garden, for tomatoes, of course. In fact, one year I beat my brother in Pennsylvania for the largest tomato by a quarter inch.

Rocks also 'grow' well in gardens there. My husband

marshaled our kids to sift the dirt in the garden so the carrots would grow straight. As adults, my kids tell that story to their children with lots of theatrical groaning.

In order to see the beautiful sites in the west, we bought a camper. This experience was fraught with dismay since my idea of camping was a Holiday Inn. The first night after the trailer was settled, my husband proudly left me to 'fix dinner' while he gathered wood for the fire pit so we could have s'mores for dessert. I had no idea how to even turn on the gas for the stove.

Some months later, on a visit to my parents, my dad asked the kids how they liked traveling. Our stalwart seven-year-old said it concisely. "Mommy cried in the camper." Nuff said?

Actually, I learned to love camping, visiting all the national parks, and just seeing the West. Our family has grown, with significant others, weddings, and now grandchildren around the table. And there was always that hot whisper in my mind, "Let me take you away from all this."

He did, in a whirlwind of love and joy. The irony? Forty years later, I still cook dinner every night.

BLESSED WITH GAS

VIRGINIA BABCOCK

Contemporary Romance

*L*acey set her keys down on her immaculate kitchen counter and opened the letter with shaky hands. She rarely received any mail but bills. Plus, this message was the first contact in two years. Having someone as eccentric as Ramona as an older sister had been harrowing for most of her life, but since the fight, there had been radio silence between the siblings. Lacey figured they were permanently estranged, but here her crazy big sister went, mailing a letter. It was even handwritten, for Pete's sake. She muttered, "And this from someone who never texts but requires me to talk on the phone or in person."

Memories of the many meals where Ramona required her to surrender her phone, which she actually locked in a lockbox until dessert, distracted Lacey for a moment. With a sigh, she unfolded the three-hole punched, lined paper. "Ramona's handwriting certainly hasn't improved since she started writing full-time. Let's hope she didn't write something as scary as her books."

Lace,

I am going to start all these letters with this information. We've never gotten along, and now we can't even be civil. Part of this is due to us always being out of sync. So, I plan to write my letters to you when it's good for me. I hope you will read them when it's good for you. I've come to realize that I've neglected to recognize you are an adult and have been for a while. I will attempt to understand if you choose to not read my letters and destroy them. I will endeavor to respect such a choice. I hope you will let me know either way.

My purpose in this letter is to apologize for arguing with you about your colon surgery. I've never had UC, so I can't possibly understand why removing most of your bowel was a viable option. Even if I can't understand your choice, I should have supported you, regardless. I am sorry.

As a peace offering, I have enclosed this food list. I recently learned that one of my college buddies had colon cancer and had most of her colon removed. I'm not trying to force you to do anything. Though, I must admit I've done so in the past. My friend's surgery was similar to yours, and today she remains healthy and active. She goes out to eat with us, and until she told me so, I did not know she used the bathroom like you do 6-8 times a day. She gave me this info when I pressed her for advice.

With hope and love,

-R

"It's called loose stools, sister of mine. Why did I think you could write 'poop?' Maybe 'number two,' 'two flushes,' or bowel movement. No, you skirted the issue. That's another problem we have. You can write the most harrowing horror, but you can't verbalize anything 'sensitive.' And, you know I hate being called Lace."

Lacey shook her head and refolded the letter. The enclosed paper was a neon green three-by-five notecard. Two sets of tiny writing filled it. Bullet points in a delicate, curvy style Lacey instantly coveted, probably the friend's writing, were surrounded by notations from Ramona. It was a list of obscure foods and food combinations.

She couldn't face reading it further. She flapped the card, fidgeting as she paced her apartment's microscopic living room. Sure, she and Ramona were usually at opposite ends of any issue, but Ramona was incredibly intelligent and often came up with genius solutions. It was her busy-body constant attempts to "fix" things that were hard to take. Plus, Lacey had started feeling a little guilty over their fight. Her sister was overbearing and self-absorbed, but she was her only sibling. Perhaps choosing not to invite her to her wedding had been a bit harsh.

A gurgle rumbled somewhere in her lower abdomen below her stomach and to the right, just above her pelvis, where lightly pressing her hand between her belly and thigh when sitting could bring relief. She could both hear and feel it. Like her ulcerative colitis, stress continued to aggravate her repaired but greatly shortened digestive system. Lacey set the letter and card down and quickly traced her well-beaten path to her bathroom. *That makes seven times before supper today.*

"YOU'RE LOOKING GOOD. There's healthy color in your cheeks, and the bags under your eyes are not as dark."

"Gee, thanks. Romantic words to make me swoon, sweetie." Lacey grimaced at her fiancé, Edward. He was using her exact terms against her, to mess with her; when he was truly concerned about her insomnia, he'd ask about her "dark circles," not "bags."

Edward raised his eyebrows and tapped the skin above her nose. "Oh, that's better! Scowl like that. Those two wrinkles creasing the skin between your eyebrows make you look so charming. They'll get permanent, you know."

Lacey grabbed his wrist and pulled his hand away.

Edward gently freed himself and then grasped her hands between both of his. "You are so easy to tease. You look beautiful as usual."

"You know, your constant teasing is hard to live with."

"I know. I can't help it."

Their budding disagreement died with a sigh. They'd had discussions about how his predilection for teasing aggravated her displeasure of being teased before and would undoubtedly do so again.

Edward smiled and rubbed her fingers.

Lacey couldn't resist the twinkles in his eyes and smiled back. Besides loving him, she appreciated his bone-deep good nature. He'd simply been born with a well-adjusted, sunny temperament. Calmness filled her like it usually did in his presence.

"So, Mom asked about the wedding breakfast. Any thoughts?"

Lacey shook her head. "No. I still don't care where or what she chooses. I won't be able to eat. You know that whatever she picks, thirty minutes after I eat it, I'll have to go, and I am not doing *that* in my dress."

Edward frowned but tried to lighten the mood. "Watching 'Bridesmaids' really got to you, didn't it?"

"I know your sister meant well and loves Kristen Wiig, but you can't tell me she truly forgot about the food poisoning scene."

"You have to admit that Maya Rudolph's squatting to crap in the middle of the street was freaking hilarious."

Lacey rolled her eyes at him. "Let's ignore the fact that I've never enjoyed 'potty humor,' but you're forgetting that I have every right to be sensitive. I didn't make it last night. Your mom kept us talking past my gurgles. After you dropped me off, I ran but messed my pants. I know getting close has only happened a few times, but honey, I've not done *that* since I was a toddler. I don't want to need adult diapers, and I need my bathroom when I need it."

"I know. I'm sorry. I'll talk to Mom."

As they finished the slices of pizza, extra thin crust, Lacey thought about Edward. He really understood her condition, but all his life, he had always dealt with emotional topics using humor and teasing. He claimed to know that she wasn't ready for jokes about her "toilet troubles" but continued to tease her out of habit.

Although, she had to give him some credit. Her long-suffering sweetheart was doing better. They shifted their habits so they did their movies before dinner, and their make-out sessions would have to wait once they got home, until after she'd used the bathroom. He'd even declared that he was practicing living her way from now on, trying to shift his own bodily functions schedule in the hope that once they were married, they would already have the "bathroom" rhythm they needed to live together.

For now, it was enough that he was willing to have separate toilets. They would share the master bath, but he'd use the toilet in the hall bath. The main bedroom's bathroom had a toilet room, and it was hers only.

"OH MY GOD. She won't let you use that toilet? You have to use the hall bathroom? That's crazy! You're paying the mortgage. You ought to put *her* in the kid's bathroom." Shemaine's jerky movements betrayed her anger. She plopped a huge plastic container on the counter. "Here's the extra turkey and potatoes with gravy. I don't know why, but Mom wants you guys to have it even after standing her up yesterday."

Edward tried to stay calm. His oldest sister won every argument and would just get nastier, but he was getting tired of his family's general inability to understand Lacey's needs.

As he tried to form a neutral reply, Shemaine continued. "... and the last slice of cake. Mom only makes her Death By Chocolate cake at Thanksgiving, and she gives the last piece to *her*." She turned to him, her hand raised to punctuate her next words.

Edward swung his arm up, palm forward to her face. "Please stop. No more. You don't understand, and I'm tired of explaining Lacey's condition to you."

"Condition. Hah. Your girlfriend is a hypochondriac and is bucking for disability. What kind of indigestion requires the removal of the colon? She doesn't even have cancer or a colostomy bag."

Edward's temper exploded. "That's it! No more. Please leave."

"What? Can't take it?"

Edward stepped forward, toe to toe and nose to nose with Shemaine. His voice was steady, his temper holding, barely. "I'm not arguing with you. I'm also not explaining this again. Your refusal to listen or even try to understand what Lacey has to live with is the height of disrespect. I'm done. Please leave."

His sister's mouth opened. He held up his hand again. She clamped her lips together and spun away. Her clomping footsteps rattled the kitchen's pendant lights. They echoed the front door slamming with a shiver before finally settling.

Edward breathed deeply. He closed his eyes and tried to regain a peaceful feeling. After telling his mother to back off her wedding plans the week earlier, his entire family had been grumbling with discontent. Lacey's face appeared in his mind, her eyes shiny with tears over their wedding. Being estranged from her only sister and orphaned when their parents died while she was in college, Lacey was grossly outnumbered and overrun by his siblings, parents, and cousins. *They hijacked the wedding breakfast and rehearsal dinner and were gunning for the ceremony.* Edward sighed. Lacey had worked hard to be especially generous with his mother. Her hard-won acceptance and the grace she regularly exhibited grounded him. Shemaine was the loudest, the top bully of his siblings. He hoped that drawing the line with her would also reset the boundaries with the rest of the crew.

His eye strayed to the card on the counter. Lacey wasn't living with him in their new house yet but would often come over for meals. She joked they were practicing family dinners, so they'd know how to behave when she moved in. The green card was from her sister. Lacey was ambivalent over whether to follow her sister's friend's advice and had forgotten the card. *Her sister is a lot like my sister when it comes to Lacey's decision to do the surgery.* He picked up the card and read it. *Could Lacey have dropped it here, subconsciously hoping I would try these things? We have been grocery shopping together.* Inspired, he opened his grocery app and started a new list.

His mom texted at that moment. More wedding suggestions. Edward frowned as he tapped out what he'd said many times over the past few weeks. His mother's "typing" ellipses blinked for what seemed like forever before her answer appeared. He read, "Son, it's Dad. Your mother accepts the conditions. She'll put on the wedding breakfast. We'll do whatever you want for the rehearsal dinner." Edward typed a quick sentence. The reply was just as fast. "Yes. You can do an open house instead of a reception. She'll get the snacks and servers, no meal."

Finally! I guess pissing off Shemaine was the right move. He'd need to have a heart-to-heart chat with his mom sometime soon, but the satisfaction of getting Lacey's wedding meals back in his fiancé's control took away the sting from his mother's anger. Mom would just have to deal.

Edward glanced at the clock and estimated Lacey's commute time before texting her. "Come over at 6? I have a surprise … Love you!" She texted back a thumbs up emoji and a kissy face.

"I WASN'T sure about the cabbage. I mean, I've done shredded cabbage on fish tacos, but never considered it as a lettuce substitute. And the ranch was awesome! Great taco salad!"

Edward nodded. "I'm glad it tasted good. Homemade ranch has less salt, and I like the tang the buttermilk brings."

"And the strawberry yogurt for dessert was refreshing." Lacey licked her spoon clean.

"Yeah, sweet, but not too sweet."

Edward reached over and grabbed Lacey's hand. "Thank you for doing a mid-week dinner with me. I just couldn't wait to tell you the good news."

She smiled, and it lit her whole face with happiness. "I appreciate what you did. I hope your mom forgives you. I don't know what to say about your sister."

"Don't worry about Shemaine. She'll cool off or not. At least it will give us something to talk about at Christmas."

Lacey laughed and hugged him.

POINTING his toes to the ceiling, Edward stretched his legs. His arms and back shifted as he contemplated getting out of bed. As usual, his first thoughts of the morning were of Lacey. The ten days until their wedding could not pass fast enough. His phone lit up. *That's what woke me.* He shifted upright and held the phone to his nose. There were a series of texts from Lacey. As he read, his smile grew wider.

"… all dark green leafy veggies are out, only cabbage, carrots, and cauliflower, especially when raw. They're my three 'Cs.' These do require fine chopping or cooking, though. Steamed or grated vegetables work too. Fried foods work in all iterations; they're slow digesting. I especially like wontons and potstickers. That's the fourth 'C' for Chinese." She continued to list the foods she now deemed "safe" to eat after experimenting.

He texted, "Awesome!" and his phone rang. "Hey, Lacey! Good morning! Love you. What's up?"

Her excitement seemed to vibrate in his ear. "Love you too! Sorry to get you up, I couldn't wait any longer. I made it through the night!"

"All night?" He knew immediately what she meant. Her periodic insomnia was worsened by multiple mid-night bathroom breaks that kept her up for a half hour each time. "Good for you!"

"Yes! First time ever since my surgery."

They kept talking, chattering like the lovebirds they were.

Suddenly, Lacey exclaimed, "Oh no!" followed by a loud rumbling sound.

Surprise filled Edward's tone. "Did you just fart?" He couldn't stifle his laughter.

Lacey cried, "Hey, it's not funny! I never fart."

"I know. Ladies don't have gas." He chuckled again. "One day you are going to poop, and I'll be there to witness it."

"Not if I can help it." She sniffed.

Edward paused, still cheerful as he pictured her face. She'd be pink and looking down at the floor with embarrassment.

"Oh, my sister's coming!" Lacey was excited again. "She texted a picture of her dress. It will go perfectly with the flowers."

Before he could reply, another burst of noise sounded. He smiled as he asked, "Again, hon?"

"Yes. It's the cabbage family doing this. Too much coleslaw."

He heard sadness in her voice. He tried to give her some hope. "Hey, isn't this a good thing? Didn't the doctor say that gas was as good as a bowel movement?"

She sighed. "Well, yeah."

"See? Take heart. This means the diet's working."

"Hopefully, but it's only been a week. And, isn't it wrong to eat yogurt for dessert?"

"You don't like eating it at breakfast, and besides, couldn't the probiotics be helping?"

"Probably. I just feel so much better overall. Eating is less of a trial, I get fewer tummy aches, and I've been going less frequently too."

"That's great news. Now we can start plotting diabolical desserts for the open house. Maybe veggie trays instead of cookies. We could use probiotic plain yogurt in the dip and get everyone passing gas."

That made her laugh. "Yes, let's!"

He couldn't help but tease her. "Do I get to share your bathroom, then?"

"Maybe. We'll have to see."

TEMPTING TRUTHS

TERRA LUFT

Urban Fantasy

*S*kylar scrubbed at the grease under her fingernails in what she'd come to think of as a futile attempt to leave the garage behind her. It would be easier to disguise it with ink from one of her gel pens. She pictured the reds and yellows peeking out from the grime and thought at least gel ink would be a reminder of something she cared about. A bright spot of good while she endured her days of doing what she had an aptitude for but didn't love.

"There you are! Been looking all over for you." Her father's booming voice startled her, and she turned to face him from the wash sink.

"Found me. Just got done with that Audi in bay one." The one Giovanni couldn't handle, and she'd saved the day on after finishing her own assigned repair. Again. She didn't bother to mention that. It would only make things worse for her friend.

"Just got another doozie in I want you to take a look at." Her father leaned on his cane, stooped and aged, eyes shining with the prospect of a challenge. It saddened her that he couldn't do the work for himself anymore, not just because he leaned on her to do it all now for him.

"It'll have to wait until tomorrow, Dad. I've got to go. It's after 3:00 already."

"Forget about it, I need you here. We don't close for another two hours."

She tossed the blue shop towel in the bin next to the sink and walked toward the door. She wasn't going to let him delay her. Not today when she had class she needed to get to. She was a grown woman, and she refused to feel like a teenager around him.

"Sorry. I have class tonight, and I've already been here a full day. We talked about this."

"You mean *you* talked about this," he said as she walked through the doorway and past him. "I never agreed to you changing things around here. You aren't the shop boss yet, young lady."

Nor will I ever be if I can help it, she thought. She was smart enough not to say that out loud, though. Instead, she walked past without saying anything and headed to the row of old lockers where her coat and bag were.

She caught the other mechanics, including Giovanni, her oldest friend, watching the exchange from behind the large window overlooking the shop floor. She shook her head slightly in his direction as if to say, not today. Like she wanted to have this discussion within view of her peers.

If she didn't leave soon, she wouldn't make it across town in time. They were learning about corset design and advanced garment structure tonight, and she'd be damned if she was going to miss it.

"Have Giovanni look at the new project, and you can fill me in tomorrow morning. If I don't leave now, I won't make it to class on time."

"Damnit, Skylar! Those classes aren't your future; this shop is."

The worry about her dad's health and the future of the family business heaped on her shoulders felt like something she could never run from, even as she ran as fast as she could toward her dreams in the fashion world. She wanted to scream. Instead, she slammed the locker shut and turned to face him.

"Never, Dad. I'm never going to give up my classes. Because fashion is what I love and what I want to do with my life. What I've always wanted to do if you'd bothered paying attention to *me* and just not what I could do for you here."

He waved his hand in her direction, like he always did when someone said something he didn't want to hear. "Pfft. This again. You're the best mechanic I've ever trained. You're meant for this, and I need you to just accept that you are taking over the family business. It's not up for negotiation!"

As if that was the only thing that mattered?

"What about what I want?"

"You're my daughter, who I love and who I thought loved me. Instead, you're abandoning me and letting me down. That isn't what family does, and you know it."

"What about Giovanni? I'm not your only option here. I don't understand why you're asking me to give up my dreams."

"Dreams? I brought you up to be a worker, not an idiot. I'm handing down to you a successful business that came from my own father, and you'd rather doodle in notebooks and pretend you're some college kid."

She noticed Giovanni standing in the doorway behind her father and briefly met his eyes. This was not a new fight, just the latest in a string of them. Giovanni was a loyal employee with an uncanny head for business, but she was the most talented with a wrench—which her father had decided meant the same as being the only option for the family business. He was a stubborn Italian with old-fashioned ideas who couldn't fathom passing on his business to someone other than family. Lucky for her, she had inherited that same stubbornness.

Giovanni's eyes reflected the same kind of anguish she felt, only she knew his was rooted in the fact that her father didn't trust him to run the business. Giovanni had been with them since he was old enough to hang around the shop. He had a brilliant mind for business and actually wanted to do it. He just didn't have the correct last name. This was not something she could control or convince her father to change his mind about. They'd been trying for years together.

She broke their eye contact with a long blink and returned her full attention to her father, the stubborn ass.

"Then I quit. Find someone else to fix cars for you who wants to do it."

THAT EVENING AFTER CLASS, Skylar walked along the path near the river. She tried to convince herself that she wasn't here specifically looking for Martin, but she knew better. It had become her routine to stop on a particular bench in the park as she made her way home. Usually, he was there already or arrived shortly after. On purpose? She hoped so, although they had never talked about it, and she didn't know if it was just coincidence for him.

Today felt different for her. The fight she'd had with her dad, and how it had escalated to a point she'd never gone to before, weighed on her mind. She could barely concentrate through an amazing design class—one she should have been riveted by. Lately, her emotions were a jumbled mess of familial guilt mixed with worry that she was being selfish. She needed someone to talk to. Not just anyone, though, she wanted a specific dark-haired someone.

She rounded the bend of the trail and saw him where she hoped he would be. The clench low in her belly, followed by butterflies at the sight of him, quickened her step, and she couldn't keep the smile from her face. She hurried even faster.

"You're on my bench again," she said, stepping off the trail, watching the late evening rays of sun glinting through the trees to highlight his bent head and bronze arms cradling his guitar. The arms she longed to have around her again.

He looked up and met her eyes, smiling to match her own grin.

"I thought we agreed it was *our* bench, and we could share it."

She let out a giant sigh and dropped down beside him. Just far enough away she wasn't touching him but close enough to feel his presence. Being with him calmed her. Sharing space with him was easy.

"Sounds like you've had a day. Want to talk about it?" He absentmindedly strummed his guitar softly, and she wondered where to begin. He had a knack for always sensing when she had things on her mind. It was one of the things that drew her to him.

"I had another fight with my dad. He laid on the family guilt, and I told him I quit. Which of course I know I can't do because that would leave him in a lurch. Why is family shit so hard to navigate?" She leaned her head back on the bench and turned to look at him, wishing he would kiss her.

"You know that the concept of 'family' is a social construct to deepen the connection of strangers who happen to share DNA, right? Our evolution has twisted it to enable parents to control their children, exactly as you're experiencing now."

"You sound like a psychology major or someone without any family at all," she laughed, wondering why they had never talked about his family much.

"You mean evolutionary biology major," he laughed. "Or I've been around and know the truth of such things?" She wondered what he was thinking about behind the intensity in his eyes.

"Whatever, I'm an art major! Besides, you don't know what it's like for me. Dad relies on me to do all the 'girl' stuff at home *plus* the shop stuff."

"I'm proud of you for standing up to him today. I know it isn't easy when he lays it on thick." He had stopped strumming the guitar and looked at her as if he could see into her soul.

"I wish I could just know what's really in my dad's heart, what's driving him to be so stubborn."

Martin reached out and brushed her hair back behind her shoulder and left his hand there, sending chills down her spine. She didn't dare move for fear it would break the moment. Feeling his touch would never get old for her.

"I doubt you'd like that. Most people have ugliness inside them where they don't hide or care about looking bad to other people," he said, sounding somehow like he had experienced this himself and lived to talk about it.

She turned a little closer toward him on the bench, reaching out to rest her hand on his knee. "Maybe. I would like to know what he's really thinking. You know, the stuff he doesn't say out loud. Even if it *is* ugly, at least I'd know the truth."

"I can show you what that's like," Martin said softly. His eyes were intense and suddenly vulnerable. She felt the air shift between them.

"Sure you can," she said, wondering what they were really talking about while her heart pounded and her skin burned where his hand still rested on her shoulder.

"I can. I'll prove it." He turned to look out across the park, moving his hand from her shoulder to hold onto his guitar again. He used his other hand, the one that had been holding the neck of the guitar, to point down the hill toward the gazebo near the playground. "See that woman in the red shirt? She's pregnant with her third child and doesn't know whether she wants to keep it because she feels overwhelmed. She's carrying the emotional well-being of her entire family and feels like she may want to just check out of all of it."

Skylar watched the woman below them, smiling at her two young children while they roughly played with each other in the grass. She looked like any other mom in the park, but was her smile just a little forced?

"Or that kid," he said, pointing again, "black hoodie, coming out of the rec center carrying the basketball. He's got what the doctors think is leukemia, but he's still trying to play on both the high school basketball and soccer teams, pretending it will all go away somehow."

"That's a great party trick, but you could be saying anything you want. It doesn't prove anything," Skylar said, wondering where he was going with this.

"Then I'll tell you what you're thinking, down here in your heart," he said, meeting her eyes again and tapping her gently once in the center of her chest.

She swallowed, thinking that if he really could tell what she was thinking, she was in trouble. "Okay," she said, trying for nonchalance as he grinned wider, and his eyes sparkled.

"Your dream of your own fashion show in Paris is not less worthy than what your father's dreams are for you with his garage."

It was uncanny. How could he know that's exactly what she'd been raging about internally as she walked through the park?

"Because I can hear what everyone around me is thinking," he said out loud in answer.

"Holy shit," she said, raising her hand to cover her mouth.

"Please don't panic."

"Oh, sure, mm-hmm," she said, eyes wide.

"You carry around a lot of guilt. Guilt about your mom leaving when you were young, guilt about not wanting to do what your dad wants now that you're grown. I know it even though you haven't ever told me about it. How else could I know those things unless what I was telling you was true?"

He looked at her calmly while she freaked out and tried not to think about anything knowing he could hear all her thoughts. Wait, he could hear *everything* she'd been thinking this whole time?

He laughed as if she'd said it out loud, and the deep sound was so unexpectedly full of delight it stopped her emotional spiral mid-freak-out. Laughter boiled out of her, too. It didn't make any sense, but she couldn't deny that this was somehow happening.

"You haven't been the only one thinking about this thing between us. I just didn't want to take advantage of the situation given my unfair abilities." He put his guitar to the side without breaking eye contact. "And yes, I would really like to kiss you again, too."

She answered by leaning in and kissing him first, grabbing a fist full of his shirt while he reached to cup the back of her neck, deepening the kiss. It was exactly as amazing as it had been every other time.

"I agree," he whispered into her mouth, smiling. "I could kiss you in the park on our bench forever."

"Not fair," she said, pulling back. "How are you doing this?"

Martin sat back and took a deep breath. "It's a lot to explain, and you probably wouldn't believe me even if I tried, but I've had these abilities for a really long time."

"Why tell me now?"

"I haven't felt like this about someone in a while, and it just makes it easier if you know everything about me. I want us to be together and build a life based on our shared dreams. I can't think of a faster way to start than to show you so that you see

120

beyond the guilt and the hang-ups you have about disappointing your dad." He shrugged with this kind of half smile that made him look vulnerable and adorable.

Her mind heard the words, but her heart felt what he was saying. If she hadn't witnessed these extraordinary powers for herself first, she would have laughed and told him he was either lying or delusional. But she couldn't argue with what he had shown her.

"Oh-kay ... go on," she said.

"I meant it. I can show you how it works. Give you a taste, so to speak. Nothing permanent. It would put you and your father on common ground and help you get through this impasse."

"How?" She had to admit the appeal. Knowing exactly what was in her father's heart would help her find a way to move past doing what he so desperately wanted her to do.

"I share my abilities with you temporarily by sharing a special kind of food. Then tomorrow, you go back to how you are now. Hopefully, with enough insight to get yourself some better boundaries when it comes to your family."

"Special food, huh? Sounds like ambrosia from mythology," she laughed. What could be stranger than him being able to read people's minds, right?

"No one's called it that in a long time," he murmured under his breath as he turned to reach into his guitar case.

She almost didn't catch what he'd said, and she shivered at his words as he pulled out a plastic container.

She took it and peeled back the lid for a peek. Mini marshmallows, coconut shavings, and pastel chunks of fruit. She looked up at him. "This is a joke, right? I eat some nasty picnic fare and get magical powers?"

"This isn't the ambrosia your grandmother used to make. That's just what your mortal mind understands when you hear the word, so it's what you see. Trust me, it tastes divine."

"Funny," she chuckled. She knew in her heart she wanted

this, so why pretend she was considering another choice? She'd think about what he meant by 'mortal' later.

"Taste it, just a bite, and I'll show you what it's like," he prompted, brandishing a fork that seemed to appear in his hand from nowhere.

"Here goes," she said, taking the fork.

Divine didn't come close to how it tasted. The most amazing flavors she couldn't place merged and blended on her tongue. She closed her eyes to savor it before swallowing.

That's when the first thought that wasn't hers hit her mind. *Here's where she's going to find out I'm not worthy of her and leaves just like all the rest before her.*

She looked at him again with wide eyes. Nothing on his face had changed, but she had heard his thoughts as plain as if he'd spoken. That wasn't all, either. Sensations rolled like waves from him and crashed into her, giving wordless glimpses of his innermost feelings. Melancholy and loneliness pulled at her heart before an onslaught of other thoughts all crowded into her from people farther away.

The pregnant woman and her screaming toddlers, the people leaving the rec center adjacent to the park, even the guy walking his dog across the bridge on the other side of the expanse of lawn all could be heard like a low din of crowd noise.

"Breathe. I know it's a lot at first. The farther away people are, the more you can shield yourself by visualizing a barrier around you. It will dull what you hear and make it manageable. With practice, you'll get used to it," he said, touching her arm tentatively. She also heard him think that he hoped she didn't pass out.

"Holy shit. You live like this?" she said, full of awe at the incredibleness of the experience. She focused on shutting out everything beyond their bench, and the din became like background chatter in a coffee shop.

"If you don't take another bite, it will only last an hour or so. If you eat the whole container, you'll have about twenty-four hours." *And oh, what an amazing day it could be.*

She smiled hearing his unspoken words sounding like his voice whispering inside her head. She hadn't expected feeling the emotions behind them, too, but she liked it. His fear and worry that this would go wrong and jeopardize what they had was a tender ball of sweetness wrapping around her. Seeing him vulnerable and as unsure as she had felt about their relationship in these early days brought them onto level ground. A place so rare for anyone. She smiled and forked another heaping bite into her mouth.

SHE DECIDED to talk to her dad first thing in the morning. It meant waking up early to catch him before he left for the garage, but it also meant fewer thoughts from other people distracting her.

She'd walked around the city with Martin until after dark, getting used to what he had given her, but she didn't have much time left if she was going to find out what was really between her and her father.

Stumbling into the kitchen, she knew Dad was already up because she could smell the first pot of coffee brewing. It was the thing they both went in search of first. She also heard the din of his thoughts, raging about how much hatred and pain there was in the world these days. She found him leaning against the counter with the morning paper spread out in front of him, mug resting nearby.

"Morning," she murmured and headed straight for the coffee pot.

Audibly, he only grunted acknowledgment of her presence. *Maybe if I don't talk to her, we won't have another fight to start the day.*

Hearing this rudeness had her scoffing, which she covered by faking a cough before she gave herself away. Did Dad leave as early as he did every morning to avoid fights with her? She felt like she'd been handed the most amazing secret of all time without enough practice last night to stay out of trouble. Martin definitely made this look easy.

With her back turned to her father, she stirred sugar into the coffee and thought about all that she'd learned last night from Martin about managing these new sensations. It felt like a life-time ago, but it'd only been six hours since she'd left him.

What Martin wanted, a life together, loomed large and promising. But first, she had to figure out if she could truly break free of her dad's expectations of how she lived her life.

She sipped her coffee and slowly turned to face where he stood ignoring her, arguing with himself about whether he should say something or if that would make things worse.

"You're up early today, especially for someone who quit her job yesterday," he said, barely glancing up at her.

"I wanted to talk to you before you left for the shop."

You mean you wanted to argue with me straight away and make my day miserable. "Yeah? Why? You takin' back what you said?"

"I feel bad about how we left things yesterday. I didn't plan to quit. You just pushed me into it like there was no other choice." She wanted to be direct and factual, and it was true, so she may as well be honest with him.

Why are broads all so damn emotional? "If you don't come back to work, I don't know how I'll keep up with all the jobs we have lined up," he said, looking down at the paper again. *And I don't want anyone to know I can't do the work like I used to.*

"Dad, I know your health is not as good as you let on these days, which is why I think it's time to make real decisions about the future of the garage. Why is it so important to you that I be the one who takes over the shop instead of appointing Giovanni, who is the best choice from a business perspective?" She sipped her coffee, looking over the rim of her mug at him.

Goddamnit, I promised my old man I'd keep the shop in the family. Giovanni ain't family, no matter what kind of a job he could do. "I don't want to fight about this. I've said my piece, and you've said yours, but your place is here doing what I say. End of story."

"Dad, just come straight with me and quit with the chauvinism and family guilt already. When you're gone, what does it matter who runs the shop? Giovanni wants it, and I don't." That should be enough for him if he loved her. She feared he still wouldn't see it for the truth that it was.

I don't care what you want, you selfish brat! "You are such a disappointment to me. I thought I taught you everything I know, including the value of hard work and doing what's right for your family." *You're just like your mother, who abandoned both of us. You're going to do the exact same thing after all I've done for you.*

He waved his hand in her direction in his typical dismissal. This time, she could hear the thoughts behind it. *You're my daughter, and what I say goes. End of story.*

His thoughts, stark and brutal even though she hadn't heard them with her ears, felt like a slap to the face. He didn't give a shit about her or what she wanted—he only cared about what she could do for him. She was done.

"You really don't care what I want or what I dream for my life." It wasn't a question because she knew the truth that was in his heart now.

"Dreams are for people who don't inherit successful family businesses, sugarplum," he said. He hadn't heard a word she'd said and was relieved that he'd won this fight. She felt it coming off him in waves, which hit her even harder than the realization of hearing exactly what he thought.

To hell with him.

"I'll give you two weeks' notice, but after that, I'm done. And I'm moving out into my own place."

THE REST of the morning at the garage was full of similar revelations. Giovanni's hidden jealousy of her because she had more talent with cars surprised her the most. She'd supported him getting the business, but she'd never known he also longed to be skilled with a wrench. All this time, she thought that he had been her biggest ally and closest friend at the shop.

By the time the effects of last night's ambrosia wore off, and she was again alone with her thoughts for company, she felt more than ready to leave this whole life behind and see where she could go on her own.

Her father was the one person who was supposed to love and support her unconditionally, yet he had lots of conditions, and not much support unless it was on his terms. She was done putting off her dreams for her life.

Martin leaned against the wall of the building next door when she left for the day. She'd been headed to the park to find him, but he had come to her instead. Knowing he had wanted to see her sooner than they usually met up had her heart soaring. She said nothing, nothing out loud anyway, but walked toward him like he was the only person she wanted to see. Because it was the truth. His smile said he knew exactly what she was feeling, as she now knew he did. The day she'd had with his gifts had given her insight into so many things.

She wished she could still hear his thoughts.

He pushed away from the wall and opened his arms toward her. She fit perfectly within the circle, head tucked under his chin. They stood there without saying anything until he finally broke the silence.

"How did the day go? Overwhelming? Enlightening?"

She could hear the hint of worry and loneliness behind his words now that she knew exactly how he felt about her and the truth of him. She also appreciated that he asked her to tell him rather than just hearing her thoughts and feeling her emotions, implying he wanted to know how she would answer. There had to be more he wasn't telling her, but she could wait to explore it. For now, the truth he'd shared opened her heart a tiny notch bigger. She had hope for a future she thought possible with him now. His arms squeezed her tighter.

"That bad, huh?" He pulled away and looked down at her. His eyes asked her to tell him everything.

"What was it you said yesterday? That 'family' is only a construct?" she chuckled, looking up into his face. "You were right. How long did it take for you to come to that conclusion?"

"I've been around a long time, and I hear a lot of things," he said.

"Thank you for today so I could know exactly how people feel about everything, even if it hurts in the short term."

He stepped back and dropped his arms, a serious look on his face.

"There's so much to talk about if we're really going to give this a shot ..." He trailed off.

She looked at him and saw the bare anguish on his face. She didn't need his abilities to know how scared he was about this.

"There's plenty of time to talk about whatever it is you're worried about." She reached up and touched his face, searching his eyes, opening herself to him and the possibilities together, full of trust.

"I'll spend whatever time we have together trying to prove I'm worthy of you," he whispered.

"That's the best part," she whispered back. "Well, that and the no-more-bullshit life."

He smiled, and she stepped closer, asking with her eyes and

her heart if she could kiss him. He smiled and met her halfway, lips parted.

THE GOOD GIRLS CHEMICAL HIGH

M. ROHR

Memoir

Christmas. Age 19.

The smiles seemed a little forced when I entered my aunt's house.

Christmas breakfast was going to be the first time my mother and I had been in the same room with each other since I ran away six months earlier.

Well, according to my mother, I ran away.

In my version of events, that fateful day started with my mom warning me that we were going to have a 'chat' when she got home from work. I sat down and sobbed after she left, knowing what that conversation would entail. The prospect of waiting all day to listen to her unleash on me for everything she thought I was doing wrong felt unbearable.

In the midst of my breakdown, I realized I didn't actually have to be there when she got home. I was eighteen. I'd graduated high school just a few days earlier. I had a job. I might have to live in my car, but that seemed phenomenally better than waiting around for another tirade about my failings.

I packed everything I could fit, stayed long enough to tell her when she got home, and left. Fortunately, I was spared from living in my car by an acquaintance from school who was moving in with her grandparents that summer. They had plenty of room and quickly became a second family to me.

When Christmas came around six months later, my family called to invite me. I knew my mom would be there, and seeing her would be unpleasant. I wanted to believe my family wanted me there, even if my mom didn't. So, I went.

At the table, I made small talk about my first semester of college with the person sitting next to me while my mom sat at the far end of the table, speaking graciously and politely with everyone but me.

An uncle said to me, "You should apologize to your mom."

"Thanks," I said. Because I'd tried to explain to him for years what life was like at home, and this was where that conversation went every time.

During clean-up, my mom and my aunt lowered their voices to speak privately. I caught snippets as I helped pass dishes to the kitchen. My mom was clearly venting about all the years she'd worked two and sometimes three jobs to give me a good life, only to have me run away in a fit of 'teenage selfishness.'

I headed to the bathroom. Alone behind the locked door, I pulled out the Oreos I'd brought for just such a moment. I sat on the floor, the familiar anticipation settling over me as I took my first bite. As the first cookie hit my taste buds, a wave of relief swept over me.

Five minutes and a half-dozen cookies later, I cleaned up and returned to the family.

Reinforced and fortified, I stayed two more hours.

In the rounds of well-wishes before leaving, my aunt gave

me a hug and whispered, "Please be kind to your mom. She loves you."

Two blocks from my aunt's house, I parked my car and retrieved donuts from the trunk. Then I leaned my seat back and released the tears I'd been holding as the first bites of fried dough melted in my mouth with a satisfaction bordering on bliss.

As I finished the first donut, the crying eased. By the end of the second, I was mostly calm. Licking the glaze of the third from my fingers, I wondered what it would be like to be happy. I ate a fourth to cheer me up.

Then, finally, the Christmas party now a distant memory, I turned the car on and started back to the home of the family I lived with, contemplating which donut to reward myself with when I got there.

WHEN MY DESCENT into addiction began, I had no access to cigarettes or drugs, alcohol in my home was closely monitored, and I didn't know anyone who would buy it for me. Any adult in my life would have noticed the smells or behaviors associated with cannabis or opiates. Such things—fortunately—weren't options.

Food, however …

Food was the perfect drug: available, socially acceptable, delicious, and the side effects of over-indulgence could be hidden with ease.

And, of course, food was universally available in my home growing up. Even more so as a young adult with a car, a job, and all the freedoms those allowed.

It began with shocking innocence: I was ten when my

parents separated, and I discovered eating and watching TV made me not so sad.

By the time I was in high school, cookies and other hyper-palatable sweets were my go-to after my mom yelled at me or I felt I'd disappointed her.

By college, I'd catch myself sneaking a fifth piece of cake into my bedroom so I could eat alone. Knowing 'normal' people didn't eat five pieces of cake, I'd convince myself to throw it out. Then I'd pace, fidget, go a little crazy in the midst of the mental insanity of a craving that I didn't understand or have the skills to cope with, then go back to retrieve the food from the trash because my brain and body were so much calmer if I just ate it.

What started as mild self-soothing in my early teens eventually became my *only* method of self-care. By high school, my solution to anything that upset me became food. Not just eating a meal but overindulgence on hyperpalatable, sugary foods until I was too ill to move.

Satiety does not apply to food addiction. A food addict loses all sense of satiety and hunger. We eat when we need a high, not when we are hungry.

We have a lot in common with smokers, alcoholics, and drug addicts: our drug of choice soothes and distracts from problematic emotions we don't know how to deal with.

Consuming an entire package of Oreos in one sitting does wonders to anesthetize guilt, anger, and stress.

I haven't tried opiates, but I've heard they do the same.

I'VE LOST jobs because I caved to a craving an hour before my shift and ended up eating uncontrollably for several hours, too ashamed to call in sick.

I failed college classes because I sat in my car watching

others walk to class sipping their coffee while I downed a clearance bakery cake.

But I wasn't obese. I didn't have diabetes. To all who cared to look, I appeared perfectly fine.

And though I didn't feel 'normal,' I also didn't perceive the danger I was in.

Food was necessary, after all. Trying to decline cake or ice cream at family or other social functions attracted protests and offense.

And the high was *nice*.

That fleeting, temporary, gratifying glimpse of physical bliss that relaxed and calmed and made me feel safe and comfortable and happy ...

It was an elusive, *glorious* thing.

And convenient.

I could get high on Thanksgiving, in a house full of people, simply by making an "I-shouldn't-but-it's-only-for-today" face and filling another bowl full of brownies or ice cream.

And I didn't regret it. There was nothing in my life that made it so easy to face my mother's displeasure than eating until I was first high and then extremely sick.

The only problem was that some of the time, I didn't *want* to eat so much.

Sometimes I ate long past self-soothing, spiraling down into a miserable and lasting discomfort accompanied by self-loathing and disgust.

The high didn't feel worth it afterward. And on increasingly frequent days, I couldn't seem to stop.

I could put food down, but I'd be so agitated and upset when I walked away, that it was only a matter of time until I returned with renewed frenzy to finish off the sugary substance I'd walked away from.

It's a special kind of hell to watch yourself doing something that hurts you and not be able to stop it.

As the eating became increasingly frequent and uncontrollable, I researched diets and self-help programs.

As I tried and failed, I inevitably ate more. It was easier to *not* try to stop because failing provoked self-loathing that led to eating in order to anesthetize the self-hatred, which led to guilt and shame, which led to more eating.

After one particularly ugly day of uncontrollable eating, I tried purging. There, kneeling in front of the toilet, trying to force myself to vomit, I had my epiphany moment: *I am not okay.*

I checked out books about eating disorders, assuming that was what was wrong. But I wasn't anorexic. I wasn't purging routinely, as is typical of bulimia. I also didn't have a struggle with body image, as the texts seemed to suggest was a fundamental symptom in both disorders.

One symptom did apply: abusing or restricting food in relation to emotional distress, which, the texts suggested, might be treated with counseling.

The first counselor told me that every day after work, he got one of his favorite chocolates from the cabinet above the fridge and ate it while he looked at his garden. He suggested that food routines, such as this, could be extremely helpful for people with eating disorders. So, I went home, made my favorite cookies, then put everything I didn't eat while I baked them into a pretty container. Then I fidgeted, twitched, and dissolved into hysterical crying while pacing the house, unable to think of anything but the cookies.

The next thing I knew, I was alone in my room, sitting on the floor and eating two at a time. I had no memory of retrieving the cookie dish. And I was *furious* someone had suggested I limit my ingestion of such sweet, lovely, happy cookies.

The second counselor gave me a copy of *Intuitive Eating* and explained that sometimes people place so many restrictions on food that they need to release all of those restrictions in order to start the healing process.

I tried that, too. I ate everything and anything. No guilt trips. No arguments. No internal battles. I gained thirty pounds in three months and lost my job because I was so physically ill all the time I couldn't get to work.

When the uncontrollable urge to eat didn't ease, I found a third counselor. After six weeks, she told me I seemed to be doing very well and that perhaps I should only come to see her once a month.

I didn't tell her I could hardly stand up because I was in so much pain after my most recent binge. Instead, I smiled, thanked her for her help, and never went back to see her again.

The continued failures to achieve any success through counseling left me with the lasting impression that I was too broken for mental health experts. If I couldn't fix me and professionals couldn't fix me, it seemed obvious nothing else could fix me, either.

IN MY MID-TWENTIES, I went to the last friend I had left: an adult child in my second family. I'd lost touch with any friends I'd made in school, either high school or college, because I was so humiliated and disturbed by the increasing frequency of the binge eating.

I told that friend I thought I had an eating disorder. The next day, he gave me a hefty stack of literature on prayer and God's power to heal.

I read it.

Then, as some Christians do, I added fasting to my prayer practice.

I lost twenty pounds in two months of fasting before I gave up and started eating again, this time with a renewed vigor I hadn't thought possible.

That son of my second family, whom I'd told about the eating disorder, told his parents what I'd said.

I overheard them talking about me.

One of them, who had become a father figure to me, said, "I wish I could tell her she's better than this, to just get over it."

In hindsight, I realize that with great familial love, a person who cared dearly for me was venting frustration that something so seemingly simple might be handicapping my happiness and potential.

At the time, the hurt of hearing that conversation felt irreparable, and I started packing to move out.

Self-help books frequently share stories of people whose bad habits stopped being a problem once they moved, changed jobs, or took a long vacation. I hoped moving would be that solution for me.

It wasn't.

I quickly discovered that renting a room in a house of college girls meant I didn't have the same need to hide my uncontrollable eating as I'd had while living with my second family. In the new place, no one noticed if I took a pizza and three milkshakes to my room. If they did, they didn't care.

And that was fine with me. Liberating, actually.

I could get high any time I wanted.

And I did.

A YEAR after moving away from my second family, I spent an entire week in my room eating, not leaving except to get more edible substances and use the bathroom.

Sick and disgusted and at a loss, I looked around for anything or anyone else who might help. I found nothing. I didn't talk to co-workers outside of work and didn't feel a close connection with any of them. I knew the names of people in my college classes but had no interaction with them outside the classroom. At church, I arrived late and left early in order to avoid exposing my shameful secret in any way. The hurt I'd felt after the reactions by my second family still stung bitterly. In my mind, counseling had been tried and proved useless.

In desperation, I went to the last person in the world who—in my mind—might have an interest in my well-being and an obligation to help save me from my hell.

"I think I have an eating disorder," I said.

My mother frowned. "What makes you *think* you have an eating disorder?"

The emphasis on the word "think" bothered me.

Before I could get past that, she said, "You don't need to look like women on TV, you know. That's not normal or healthy."

It seemed so obvious to me that this had nothing—*nothing*—to do with the stereotypical misunderstandings of anorexia and bulimia that I had no response. I hadn't considered how I would describe the problem. I wasn't going to tell anyone that sometimes I came to after a binge only to find myself lying on my bedroom floor next to empty food packages having no memory of eating them.

I was so ashamed of it that I couldn't describe the symptoms. Couldn't even begin to formulate a sentence that would describe my hell.

"How's school?" my mom asked, changing the subject to bring our dinner conversation back to something more 'normal.'

Grateful for the change of topic, I told her about my classes and then spun an acceptable tale about the social events I'd attended.

I hadn't actually gone to any social events. I'd get twitchy and agitated in any situation involving food. Like the proverbial "little kid in a candy store" insanity but on steroids and laced with the paranoid rapidity characteristic of a cocaine addict in need of a hit.

So instead of socializing, I sat alone in my bedroom and ate.

Well, not *alone*.

I had my food with me.

A RECOVERING alcoholic once described alcohol as her soul mate. That's exactly how I felt about food.

In my mind, I'd tried every option I was aware of: counseling, telling a friend and then my second family, and, finally, trying to talk to my mom about it.

I stopped trying to fix whatever it was that was wrong with me and surrendered—utterly and completely. Life became nothing more than a calculation between the previous binge and how long it would be until I got my next one. There was no joy or happiness or laughter unless it was with food. No sadness or sorrow unless it was a lack of food.

While my days spiraled into a roller coaster of emotion and cravings based on how long it had been since my previous high and how long until I could get my next, I got nearly straight A's and paid my own way through college. I paid my bills, went to church, helped elderly neighbors, and made appropriate appearances at family events.

None of it meant anything.

It was like watching someone else live my life—the conver-

THE GOOD GIRLS CHEMICAL HIGH

sations I had, the people I interacted with—all of it was someone else using my body to go through the necessary motions. Meaning only existed when I ate.

My highs were my lovers and my friends.

When I was lonely, I found companionship in food. When I was sad, solace came only from eating.

No one understood my misery—except food. No shared happiness with me—except food.

Food calmed the madness, the guilt, the shame. It took away the pain.

Food didn't judge me. Didn't tell me I should be better. Didn't tell me to stop trying to be something I wasn't. Food was kind, gentle, and understanding. Food didn't hurt my feelings. Food stayed with me when I felt lonely. Food was never too busy or distracted. Food gave me its undivided attention. Food provided devoted affection.

It was, as that woman described, the perfect soul mate.

IN CHURCH ONE DAY, a woman shared her experience overcoming an addiction to opiates. At its worst, she said, her life had been nothing but a calculation between how long since the last high and how long until the next. Nothing else existed. She maintained a marriage, raised three kids, worked part-time, and participated in community service … all the while caring about absolutely nothing except when she could get her next pill.

That was *me*.

The years of isolation shattered. I wasn't having a mental breakdown. I wasn't unfixable. Eating disorder treatments hadn't helped because I didn't have an eating disorder.

I was an addict.

I found that woman after the service and started sobbing before I could even say hello.

She wrapped her arms around me and whispered, "I know, sweetheart. I know."

THREE DAYS LATER, I drove nearly forty minutes from home to ensure no one recognized me when I attended my first recovery meeting. The woman from church had invited me to her meeting, but I'd declined. I didn't even want to be in the same space as anyone familiar for this first meeting.

A quick survey of the half dozen people in the semi-circle led me to sit between a small, timid-looking man, probably in his early fifties, and a soccer mom in knee-length shorts sporting light makeup and a ponytail.

The meeting started. The facilitators introduced themselves, explained the meeting format, and told me I could say "pass" if I didn't want to participate.

After the reading portion of the meeting, the soccer mom to my left shared about a decade of shooting heroin into her veins between her kids' sports and music practices. Her husband didn't know. Her family thought she was meeting with a book club.

Next, the man to my right shared about nearly forty years fighting the addiction that brought him recovery. Based on a few of his vague comments, I quickly realized I was sitting next to a person who had, in the throes of sexual addiction, committed heinous crimes.

The facilitators asked me if I'd like to share.

Yeah right.

What would I say?

"Hi, I eat cookies."

No f***ing way.

Those people had *serious* challenges. I just needed to stop eating so much.

I left the meeting promising myself I'd never overeat again.

That week was a brutal awakening as I paid attention, for the first time in years, to what my daily life consisted of.

Every day that week, I woke up sick and miserable from the previous day's binge and knew that within hours I'd be watching myself eat until I was in physical and emotional agony. I couldn't stop it. I hated it. I hated myself. I hated every second I was alive.

Dear God, I thought, reciting the only prayer I had left, *Please don't make me live another day.*

I bought ice cream on my way to the meeting the following week.

The next week, I did the same.

AFTER SIX MONTHS of sitting quietly in those recovery meetings, I overcame the embarrassment of introducing myself to 'real' addicts.

"Would you like to share this week?" asked the woman leading the meeting.

"Hi," I said. "I'm an addict. I ... have an eating disorder."

"Welcome," the group said in unison, as is the 12-step custom.

No one laughed or made a face when I said *eating disorder*.

After the meeting, the facilitator told me her daughter had a similar struggle. It started when her parents divorced, and she began eating her feelings because she didn't know how to cope with them. The facilitator gave me her phone number and invited me to call so we could chat one-on-one.

For the first time in years, the chasm between me and the outside world had been bridged. Someone *knew* me. Knew what was wrong. Didn't despise me because of it.

As we walked out, the facilitator told me the title of a book her daughter had found helpful. "It was the best we found on food addiction," she said.

Food addiction.

Finally—*finally*—my nightmare had a name.

I cried all the way home.

FOOD IS SOMETIMES REFERRED to as a good girl's chemical high. The name isn't just apt, it's quite perfect.

Drugs weren't available to me, but hyperpalatable foods, particularly sugary ones, provided a sensory experience leading to a dopamine response which numbed feelings of stress. The relief became a high. A cue-reward cycle began, and I became dependent.

Part of the tragedy of the last twenty years is how different they might have been if I'd latched on to alcohol or cigarettes or prescription painkillers instead of food. I can't help but assume my attempts to ask for help would have had very different outcomes.

With that in mind, I've worked hard to find the courage to share a little of my experience with people in my church congregation, with ecclesiastical leaders, with twelve-step meetings, and with friends who are parents.

"If you're the kind of parent who talks to your kids about drugs," I tell them, "then talk to them about food, too."

As with any compulsive substance or behavior, early awareness is key.

Several times, after speaking with groups about my experience with addiction and recovery, someone has come up to me afterward, crying so hard they can't introduce themselves or explain.

Like the woman so many years ago did for me, I hug them as tight as I possibly can, tell them I understand, and ask if they'll come to a meeting.

Christmas. Age 37.

MY HUSBAND, kids, and I arrive as breakfast is set out. I make the rounds giving hugs, then make my way to the kitchen, where I find a small space for the crockpot I brought with a favorite dish of mine. It's a crockpot chocolate cake made with avocados, almond flour, and honey. Yes, I'm planning to eat chocolate cake for Christmas breakfast. It's sweet, and I think of it as a treat, but there's nothing in it that is addictive to me. It is "safe."

I started preparing myself for this day almost two months ago. Around the middle of October, I stopped anything that could be stopped: work projects, house projects, self-improvement projects, homemaking projects. I emailed all the distant relatives, told them happy holidays, then gave myself permission to not answer calls, emails, or texts until January.

We've been eating off disposable dishes for nearly a week to minimize kitchen clean-up. I made freezer meals, too, so I wouldn't have to cook for most of December. I purchased extra linens and kids' clothes from a thrift store so that we can simply toss the used stuff in the laundry room and pull out clean ones. I'll deal with it in January.

This is my self-care bubble.

Most importantly, any edible substance in my house that

might possibly be problematic for me over the holidays was either discarded or given away.

Over the course of Christmas morning, some of my extended family ask why I'm not eating the toxic substances they've brought. I give vague but firm answers about dietary preferences. I've practiced those responses in front of a mirror.

I sit as far away from the buffet as I can and try not to look at it. I get agitated because I know it's there. I take long breaks in the bathroom—*without* edible substances—for deep breathing and centering.

After two hours, I give my husband the signal that I can't be here anymore.

When we get in the car, I close my eyes and cry—whether from relief at success or misery at leaving behind that buffet of sweet and intoxicating bliss, I'm not sure.

Right now, it doesn't matter.

I did what I'd set out to do: my first Christmas sober in almost twenty years.

Made in the USA
Columbia, SC
06 December 2023

27870120R10085